DEDICATION

♛ ♛ ♛

To my husband Todd
for his constant love and support.

ACKNOWLEDGEMENTS

※ ※ ※

Many thanks to the authors cited in the selected bibliography. Without their extensive research, this fictional portrayal of the events surrounding the raid of Fort William and Mary would not have been possible.

In particular I want to thank Thomas F. Kehr, Esq., a former president, historian and member of the New Hampshire Society of the Sons of the American Revolution and author of *"The Seizure of His Majesty's Fort William and Mary at New Castle, New Hampshire, December 14-15, 1774."*

Not only did Mr. Kehr's meticulously researched and documented article about the raid at the fort form the basis for this story, his willingness to review my manuscript and provide detailed information and insights was invaluable. I am truly grateful for all the time he spent helping me to understand the complexities of the Piscataqua region in 1774 and for his encouragement with this project.

PREFACE

꧇ ꧇ ꧇

The Portsmouth Alarm: December 1774 is based on a real event. In the months prior to December, the tensions between the British government and the colonists reached a boiling point after Parliament blockaded Boston Harbor and enacted other restrictive measures, known as the Intolerable Acts, as a punishment for the event later known as the Boston Tea Party.

Alarmed by the harsh response by the British government to the dumping of tea into Boston Harbor, the colonies called for a Continental Congress, composed of delegates from the colonies, to meet in Philadelphia to decide a course of action. The Continental Congress proposed a boycott of all imports from Britain in hopes that the economic hardship would force the government to change its policies. However, it is important to note that few advocated independence from Britain at the time.

The Continental Congress also supported the creation of committees of correspondence for easy communication between and within colonies, and proposed the creation of committees of inspection to ensure the recommended boycott was followed. Some colonies had already formed these committees.

As stated, the Portsmouth Alarm was an actual event. Three main characters, Andrew Beckett, Jack Cochran and Joseph Reed are fictional, but all other named individuals are real people who lived during the turbulent time in December 1774.

I have tried to keep all characters' actions and words consistent with my interpretation of the historical information I have reviewed, but the book should be read as a work of fiction.

BOSTON, PROVINCE OF MASSACHUSETTS
GREEN DRAGON TAVERN
December 12, 1774 — 9:00 P.M.

☙ ☙ ☙

Four men huddled at a small corner table inside the Green Dragon Tavern on Union Street. Some were members of the committee of correspondence. Others were members of an association created to watch the movements of the British soldiers and those who supported royal policies. A fire warmed the room, but the men wore wool coats. There was no need to remove them. They would not tarry long in the tavern.

As usual the establishment was crowded. Most of the tavern regulars were supporters of the movement to resist the so-called Intolerable Acts. But despite the comfort of supporters in the tavern, the men at the corner table took care not to be overheard. General Thomas Gage, the governor of Massachusetts, had his spies so the men spoke quietly, on their guard.

This night the men did not perform their regular ritual of swearing on a Bible, promising to keep all matters discussed during their meeting a secret from all except a select group that included John Hancock, Sam Adams, Joseph Warren, Benjamin Church and one or two others. It wasn't necessary. The information being discussed would be acted upon this night or not at all. Time was critical.

The men had assembled quickly at the tavern after receiving intelligence about General Gage's current plan. The information they were given was shocking and the plan was already in motion. If the men seated at the table didn't act tonight, it would be too late.

The group's leader Paul Revere, a silversmith by trade, sat facing the door, monitoring the comings and goings of the tavern patrons. He sipped from a tankard as he drummed the fingers of his left hand on the table, growing impatient with the indecisiveness of the others.

"We must do something!" Revere spoke through gritted teeth. "We have to warn the committee in Portsmouth!"

Revere was still furious that the citizens of Boston had been caught off guard in September, just a few months earlier. Gage had ordered the seizure of gunpowder stored at the Provincial Powder House about six miles northwest of Boston. Under cover of darkness, the powder was removed by Gage's soldiers and taken to Castle William in Boston Harbor.

When the people discovered the province had been robbed of its powder, the town went into panic. Rumors flew that men were killed, that regulars were marching and that the King's ships were attacking Boston. None of those rumors proved to be true, but the precious powder was lost. That's when Paul Revere vowed that nothing like that would ever happen again.

Revere, a sturdy dark-haired man, set down his tankard with a thud. "A decision has to be made now." His deep brown eyes moved from man to man. "We are running out of time."

William Cooper, the clerk of the committee said, "I agree with Paul. I fear the consequences of not acting will not only put the entire Piscataqua region at the mercy of the royal government, but will put all of us at risk."

Cooper continued, "Despite our best efforts, it is clear we cannot get the required seven members of the committee together before to-morrow night." He leaned forward in the straight wooden chair. "Waiting until we can convene a large enough group to make the de-cision will be too late to warn the people in New Hampshire and northern Massachusetts."

Revere spoke up. "If I am to travel to Portsmouth, I must leave Boston before first light. Travel will be brutal. The roads are rutted with ice. We can't wait. We have to act without the required seven members."

The men sat in silence.

It was a difficult decision. No less than seven members of the committee of correspondence were needed to take any action. It was a requirement to safeguard against mistakes or misuse of the system, but it was not always easy to assemble the required number of men, especially when decisions had to be made quickly.

Revere broke the silence, "I don't think we have a choice."

Each man gave a nod of agreement. The decision was made.

"Paul," Cooper told Revere, "you will need to get the information to a man named Samuel Cutts. He is a member of the committee of correspondence in Portsmouth, New Hampshire."

PORTSMOUTH

PROVINCE OF NEW HAMPSHIRE
LATIN GRAMMAR SCHOOL
December 13, 1774 — 11:20 A.M.

Andrew looked away from the Latin passage on his desk, blinking his hazel eyes now red and scratchy from the dry air in the room. The schoolroom was quiet except for the crackle of the fire and an occasional cough. The schoolmaster, Major Samuel Hale, sat at a large wooden desk at the front of the room reading a book.

Most of the boys intently eyed the work before them. But Charles, legs stretched out and ankles crossed, looked relaxed — even bored. At eleven, he was three years younger than Andrew, but could parse and construe Latin as if it was the first language he'd learned. His father, Dr. Cutter, practiced medicine in town and helped Charles with his Latin.

Charles glanced up, caught Andrew's gaze and smiled smugly. They both knew Charles understood the passages better than Andrew, but Andrew had no help at home. He was the first in his family to ever attend the Latin Grammar School. It was open to any boy who wanted to further his education and position and Andrew hoped to become a doctor.

Upon Major Hale's recommendation, Charles's father had agreed to let Andrew study medicine with him after he attended Harvard College. Andrew planned to sit for Harvard's entrance exam in the upcoming summer. Major Hale said it was time, and it was common knowledge that if Major Hale said you were ready to apply for entrance to Harvard, you were ready. But every time Andrew thought about it he felt an ache in the pit of his stomach.

He turned back to the Latin passage determined to make sense of the words. As his schoolmaster always said, "diligentia maximum etiam mediocris ingeni subsidium." In Latin it means diligence is a very great help even to a mediocre intelligence.

Two quick raps on the door broke Andrew's concentration and stole the attention of every boy in the room. Major Hale leapt up from his heavy wooden chair as if he was one of the boys rushing from the schoolroom upon dismissal.

All eyes moved in unison following his steps. Such an interruption was extremely rare. The Latin Grammar School, considered among the best preparatory schools in New England, was a place for serious study. Uninvited visitors were not welcome.

Major Hale stepped outside closing the warped wooden door the best he could, deliberately insuring privacy.

All eyes now searched one another's. Latin passages were forgotten.

"Jack," A voice whispered sharply to Jack Cochran seated in the front row closest to the door. "Did you see who it is?"

Jack turned part way 'round in his chair. Only his thin, fine-featured profile visible, he whispered back, "I couldn't see."

Jack always sat by the door as if standing guard. He told anyone who would listen that he would rather serve full time in the militia than be a student at the Latin Grammar School, but at thirteen he was too young. His father, Captain John Cochran, was the militia officer in charge at the fort, His Majesty's Castle William and Mary on neighboring Great Island in the Town of New Castle. Andrew was certain that one day Jack would hold that post.

Standing up, Jack eased his lanky frame to the side window closest to the door. The dry wood floor cracked with each step. Quickly craning his head forward, sneaking a peek out the window, he dropped into his chair and declared, "A man, medium height, but his tricorn is pulled down so low I couldn't see his face."

"It must have something to do with one of the committees," Charles's voice boomed in the silent room. He sat up straight, no longer bored.

Several other boys nodded. Andrew, too. It was difficult to imagine any other reason for a disruption of studies.

A number of committees had been established in Portsmouth in the last months. One was a committee of correspondence, set up to communicate with other towns in New Hampshire and with the other colonies.

Another was the Portsmouth Committee of Forty-Five, a committee of forty-five members including their schoolmaster. Some called it a committee of ways and means, but the purpose was to keep order and quiet in the town.

And a Committee of Twenty-Five was formed to make sure the boycott of British goods was enforced. On the first of December, just a couple of weeks earlier, the town officials had agreed to follow the Continental Congress's recommendation to boycott all British goods as a protest against the actions taken by the British government against Boston.

This new boycott of all British goods, was in addition to the boycott of tea. The town had already been boycotting tea for several months in protest of the tea tax enacted by Parliament.

Many of the boys exchanged sly smiles, excited by the possibility of trouble.

But, Andrew did not share their excitement. He didn't want any of the trouble brewing to interrupt his schooling. He needed to be ready to take the entrance exam for Harvard College in the upcoming summer. All of his future plans depended on it.

Jack slipped out of his seat again, grimacing with each crack of a floorboard. He tilted his head close to the door, listening. Suddenly he jumped back, rocking the chair as he dumped his frame into it.

The chair had barely returned to its four legs when the door swung open and Major Hale, with lips pursed and eyebrows knitted tight, stepped back into the classroom.

It was at that brief moment, with the door still open, a distant sound floated into the schoolroom. The Major closed the door quickly, but not before an alarm was sounded by one of the boys.

"Drums! Drums in the street!"

With that cry, the room exploded, chairs fell to the floor as boys

15

leapt to their feet to answer the call. Andrew jumped up, too. His pulse pounded in his ears. He didn't want trouble, but was prepared to answer a call for help if he was needed. He was, after all, a loyal citizen of the province of New Hampshire.

"Stop!" Major Hale shouted.

The boys froze. Major Hale rarely raised his voice. It wasn't necessary. His kindness and knowledge commanded respect from his students that a raised voice never would.

"There are no drums beating! No one is calling out an alarm! Sit down!"

Righting chairs in a rapid but deafening chaos, the boys sat down. Eyes forward, no one uttered a sound. Andrew's heart was still pounding.

Major Hale took a deep breath and exhaled before he spoke. "There is a problem that I must attend to immediately." His voice was firm, but even in tone.

"Complete your readings. Then you are dismissed for the day."

No one dared ask his business. But every boy in the room knew Major Hale was a member of the Committee of Forty-five, even though he never spoke of it at school.

"Jack," Major Hale said, "See to the fire before you leave."

Major Hale did not bother to gather his belongings before he hurried out of the schoolroom.

The boys tripped over each other scrambling from the classroom. Some of the older, bigger ones pushed the others aside. Andrew, tall and broad for his age, did not get jostled.

Major Hale climbed into a waiting carriage. He barely sat down when the driver whistled and the horse set out at an urgent pace.

Shouts came from the boys left standing on King Street.

"They're headed to the wharf!"

"Trouble at the wharf!"

"A ship must be entering the harbor loaded with British goods!"

"Maybe tea!"

Andrew stared at the carriage weaving down the rutted road. Trouble at the wharf was likely with the non-importation policy in effect. It could be tea, but now it could be any goods.

"If it's tea," Charles said, "no one will believe Mr. Parry this time!"

Laughter erupted at the thought.

It was true. How could anyone believe Edward Parry didn't know tea was coming for a third time? In the last six months, two shipments of tea had arrived in Portsmouth after the town had agreed not to import any tea in protest of British policy to tax it. Both tea shipments had been consigned to the local merchant named Edward Parry, and both times he claimed to have no knowledge that shipments were coming to him.

Standing in the street in the frigid cold, the boys argued back and forth about how a new tea shipment would be handled.

"They'll land it and reship it, again."

"No! No! Let's go to Parry's house!" one boy yelled. "Maybe they'll break the windows like last time!"

Andrew recalled that night. Boys threw stones and battered the shutters breaking windows of the Parry house. The unsettling memory had stayed with Andrew. Portsmouth was usually a very peaceful and orderly town.

Jack slammed the schoolhouse door and hurried down the steps, joining the boys on the street. He held a book in one hand and told them, "I don't think it's about tea." His intense brown eyes moved from boy to boy.

Andrew respected Jack — liked him, too. They often studied together. Soft spoken but direct, Jack had a welcoming smile and even temper. The boys let him speak.

"I'd have heard about another tea shipment. The governor told my father about the two previous shipments before they arrived. He needed the militia soldiers' help with protecting the tea. Governor Wentworth would definitely ask my father for help if tea was landed again."

"You haven't been home, maybe this just happened or maybe the governor didn't know," a tall boy challenged.

Jack pursed his lips. "Maybe. But I don't think so. The governor usually hears about shipments in advance."

While attending school, Jack stayed with his grandparents in town during the week, going home to the fort only on the weekends. Today was Tuesday.

"It doesn't matter. You can't trust the governor!" Another boy challenged.

Andrew stiffened, irritated by the comment.

A low grumble of agreement sliced through the group separating those who still trusted the governor from those who no longer did.

Jack's eyes flashed in quick anger — unusual for him. Then he bit his lower lip and said nothing more.

Jack's father, Captain Cochran, as the officer in charge of the fort, had always been a supporter of the royal governor. Jack was a supporter, too. And for almost seven years the governor had been very popular with most of the citizens, but some now questioned Governor Wentworth's loyalty to the people of New Hampshire.

Andrew looked at Charles, wondering if he would try to protect the governor. Dr. Cutter and Governor Wentworth were long-time friends. Other boys also looked at Charles for a word or a sign, but he remained silent.

"Why are we standing here?" a husky boy broke in. "Even if it isn't tea, there could still be trouble!"

"Let's go!" another agreed.

"To the wharf!"

PORTSMOUTH WHARF
11:50 A.M.

🐚 🐚 🐚

Pain shot up Andrew's left shin as his thin leather-soled shoes pounded the uneven road. Snow had come early this year — in November. After a brief thaw and refreeze, the roads were now rutted with frozen mud.

Andrew barely kept pace with the boys in his class. Despite being taller than most, they ran on excitement that Andrew did not share. Jack Cochran ran next to him in silence, his chiseled face taut. Charles lagged behind the group headed to the wharf.

Boys hooted and shoved each other. A few whooped like Indians and shouted, "Remember Boston!"

Andrew watched a frown cross Jack's face.

Six months after men in Boston threw a shipment of tea overboard, the British government retaliated by closing off commerce in Boston Harbor and dismantling the provincial government in Massachusetts.

Now many believed Portsmouth would be next unless the citizens submitted to all of the royal policies — fair or not. Some said it was just a matter of time until the harbor in Portsmouth would be closed just like in Boston. They said Parliament was looking for a reason to close the harbor.

If any goods were landing today, there could be trouble. If Edward Parry had tea shipped again, even Andrew was certain there would be trouble — big trouble. And if there was trouble, he knew it could give the British government the reason it was looking for to close the port in Portsmouth.

Reaching the waterfront, Andrew stopped short. Charles rammed straight into him from behind and was knocked off his feet.

"Watch what you're doing!" Charles complained as he jumped up, his face scarlet.

Two boys laughed at him, and Charles pushed a boy who had to stagger to maintain his balance.

Andrew looked out over the water. The sails of Piscataqua ships dotted the harbor even at this time of year. The Piscataqua River ran faster than most any river in the world, keeping the harbor open despite freezing temperatures. New Hampshire didn't produce enough food to feed her people, but her treasure, lumber, was always in demand.

New Hampshire timber was among the best in the colonies. The tall white pine provided masts for the British Navy. Other timber was carried to the "Sugar Islands" to build houses and barrel products. From England, the ships often carried home shipbuilding supplies and manufactured goods. Ships returning from the West Indies were full of sugar, molasses, coffee and rum.

Ships from Portsmouth also engaged in a triangular trade. Lumber and fish sailed to the West Indies, then sugar from the Indies sailed to England. The ship would then return to Portsmouth with English goods, or the ship was sold in England and the captain would book passage home on another ship.

Andrew pulled his eyes from the water. The smell of salt was in the air as the wind blew onshore. His eyes followed what his ears heard — loud voices.

The crowd was small, too small, he reasoned, to protest a tea shipment. News of a tea shipment would have blown through town in short time and the wharf would be crowded with angry protesters. But something was happening. There was a commotion at the far end of the wharf. Men were shouting and crowding together.

All of a sudden he heard . . . SPLASH!

Andrew sucked in a breath, recoiling at the thought of falling into the freezing water of the Piscataqua!

Then he heard . . . . Was it thunder?

Jack and Charles both pointed in the direction of the sound, shouting in unison, "Look!"

Andrew couldn't believe what he saw. Running toward them, hooves pounding like thunder, were sheep! There must have been fifty of them!

There was another splash as a man was pushed off the wharf, sideswiped by the stampede. Andrew watched a different man jump into the frigid Piscataqua to avoid being trampled.

Now the sheep were coming right at Andrew and the other boys!

The boys scattered, running in all directions. Andrew jumped to the side at the last moment, barely escaping a wild-eyed ewe that veered suddenly toward him.

Charles, now next to him, laughed so hard his blue eyes watered.

Andrew saw men run down the wharf as they tried to herd the sheep back together. Some of the boys from his class helped. Andrew watched Jack Cochran wave his arms, book in one hand, trying to contain the herd.

After several moments Jack yelped and jumped on one foot. He stood for a moment with shoulders hunched and head down before he slowly limped over to Andrew and Charles.

Jack grumbled as he sat down on a barrel, "Stupid sheep stepped on my foot!" He slid his foot out of his shoe and rubbed it with both hands.

Still laughing, Charles now wiped tears running down his cheeks.

Jack glared at him. "I hope your eyes freeze shut! That hurt!"

Andrew smiled. He looked back toward the wharf and saw a familiar face. His friend, Joseph Reed, was walking toward them.

"Drew!" It was Joseph's voice. Andrew winced at the familiar childhood name. He'd asked Joseph many times to call him Andrew, but his requests were ignored.

Round faced and thickly built, Joseph had a scowl on his face. It was an increasingly common expression.

They had been friends for as long as Andrew could remember. Andrew's father shipped barrels, and staves — the strips used to make them, on Joseph's father's ship the *Voyager*, mainly to other colonies and the West Indies. But trade was difficult these days, not only due to the restrictions imposed by Parliament, but now because of the boycott. Making matters worse, Captain Reed was still at sea.

"What are you doing here?" Joseph eyed Jack and Charles, but spoke to Andrew.

Andrew nodded toward a group of men that included Major Hale, but asked, "Any word on the *Voyager*?"

Joseph shook his head and Andrew fell silent. He knew Joseph was worried. The *Voyager* was overdue. His father had hoped to bring in another shipment of goods prior to the boycott going into effect. There could be many reasons for the delay, but most of them weren't good. Bad weather was a real possibility. So was an unwelcome encounter with another vessel.

Regardless, if the *Voyager* had loaded British goods and then experienced difficulty that would delay the arrival, they would have to return to England, find another buyer for the goods or dump the cargo. Andrew was certain that Captain Reed would not bring British goods into Portsmouth Harbor now that the boycott was in effect, but sailing back in ballast was not acceptable, either.

Charles blurted out, "What's going on?" Charles's small frame shook as he fired questions at Joseph. "Why was the Committee of Forty-Five called out?"

Andrew wished he could will Charles away. Charles could unwittingly leak information Andrew wanted to keep from Joseph.

"Captain Chivers is trying to sail to the West Indies with fifty sheep!" Joseph's scowl deepened as he looked back to the wharf.

Andrew followed his eyes. The sheep had been herded back together and were now calm.

"The committee was called out for the sheep?" Charles's slight shoulders sank with disappointment.

"Told you it wasn't a tea shipment," Jack declared.

Charles shrugged. "Well, I was right about the Committee of Forty-Five."

"I wish it had been tea," Joseph said. "I would be first on board to toss the filthy weeds into the harbor."

Charles scoffed at the idea. "Throwing the tea overboard in Boston didn't make any sense."

Joseph's body stiffened and his eyes grew wide. He stepped forward, towering over the eleven year old. "The men in Boston had to do it! They had to take a stand! The British government has no right to tax us on tea or any goods. We're not represented in Parliament. We have our own assembly."

"But throwing the tea in the harbor just made Parliament angry." Charles countered. "Now Parliament closed the port in Boston until someone pays for the destroyed tea. It would have been cheaper to pay the tax. Besides, the taxed tea is actually cheaper than the tea we were buying before."

Joseph's voice rose. "But it would be wrong to pay the tax even if it's cheaper!"

It was a complicated issue in a lot of minds — including Andrew's. Most were convinced that Britain was stepping on the colonists' rights in order to raise revenue and thought the tea tax should not be paid. But not all supported throwing the tea into Boston Harbor. Some described it as a needless destruction of private property. Andrew believed the support being shown for Boston was more about Britain's severe retaliation for the event rather than agreement with the act of dumping tea into the harbor.

Charles shrugged essentially dismissing Joseph's argument. "So what's wrong with sending sheep to the Indies?" Charles asked. "I thought importing was banned not exporting."

"Not sheep!" Joseph half snarled. "The non-exportation provision hasn't gone into effect yet, but the Continental Congress has prohibited exporting sheep abroad. We need the wool so we don't have to depend on Britain for our clothing." Under his breath Joseph muttered, "At least they did that much."

Joseph had made it clear that in his mind the Continental Congress had not done enough. The policy of non-importation had gone into effect, but export trade had not yet been formally banned. If Boston Harbor didn't reopen by September, exports to Britain would likely be banned as well. But that wasn't soon enough for Joseph.

Despite it hurting his family, Joseph believed a total ban was the only way to coerce the government into easing up on restrictions. A similar boycott had worked years ago to get the British government to repeal an unfair policy called the Stamp Act.

Jack said, "Since the excitement is over I need to head to the State House to pick up documents for my father and then go home." He glanced up at the cloudy sky. "It looks like it will snow soon."

Charles said, "Feels like it too."

"Home? On a Tuesday?" Andrew was surprised.

"My grandfather is coming to the fort for a visit. It has been a long time since I have seen him."

Charles said, "I thought you lived in town with your grandparents during the week."

"Those are my mother's parents. My father's parents live inland in Londonderry."

Jack's smile evaporated as he held up the book in his hand. "But Major Hale made sure I have an assignment." With a wave, Jack turned and began the walk to the State House at the Portsmouth Parade, his limp barely noticeable.

Charles said, "Well if there isn't any tea, I'm going home."

Andrew placed a hand on his shoulder and walked a few steps with Charles, speaking softly. "I'll see you at your house."

Still walking, Charles pressed his lips into a straight smirk. "Hannah will be wearing her finest dress."

"I'll be there." Andrew gave Charles a nudge to move him along.

Andrew glanced over at Joseph hoping he wasn't paying attention to Charles, but he was.

Charles walked a few steps backward as if he would say more. Then, to Andrew's relief, Charles turned around and started down the street.

"Andrew!" Charles suddenly called over his shoulder as he ran. "Don't be late! Governor and Mrs. Wentworth will arrive promptly at 2:00."

Andrew turned and Joseph had crossed the few steps between them in an instant. His face was inches from Andrew's.

PORTSMOUTH WHARF
12:10 P.M.

"You're spending the afternoon with Dr. Cutter and Wentworth?" Joseph's eyes blazed with sudden anger.

Andrew braced for the verbal fight he had hoped to avoid. Joseph had no tolerance for the province's royal governor.

"You know my family isn't here. I have to eat."

Andrew's parents, older brother and younger sister had left that morning to visit his uncle's home, located several miles inland, just as they did every year at this time. Andrew's father was a cooper, one of Portsmouth's best barrel makers. While there, his father, brother and uncle would cut down trees for the wood needed to make the barrels and casks he crafted so expertly. Winter is a good time to fell trees. The snow pack breaks the fall leaving the precious wood undamaged. Andrew stayed home, not wanting to miss any days at school.

"You don't have to eat with *him*." Joseph challenged.

Him meant the province's royal governor. Andrew knew he had

28

no chance of changing Joseph's opinion about Governor Wentworth, so he quickly added, "I don't want to be late."

Andrew immediately dug in his heels and hurried down the street. Joseph should be happy for him, he thought. This dinner was about his future. And Hannah, Charles's sister, would be there. Joseph knew how Andrew felt about her.

He kept walking, lengthening his stride. He hoped his uncharacteristic abruptness had stopped Joseph, but, he heard footsteps, behind him, coming closer.

Andrew didn't slow down. Instead, he picked up the pace. Joseph would have to struggle to catch up. Joseph's legs were shorter, despite being a year older. But within moments he fell into step beside Andrew.

"I'm asking again, Andrew, how can you spend time with Wentworth?"

It was not lost on Andrew that Joseph did not give Governor Wentworth the respect of calling him by his title.

Andrew stopped and turned to Joseph. He held his temper by taking in a deep breath of cold air. "You know very well that I would not turn down an invitation to dine with the Cutter family. I'll be living with them while I study medicine. Dr. Cutter thought I would enjoy talking about his days at Harvard since I will apply for admission this summer."

"But, Wentworth will be there!" Joseph spat out the words as if to rid his mouth of something distasteful.

They stood in the street — now eye to eye. Andrew's frustration mounting. Dr. Cutter, Harvard College, they were important to Andrew. He didn't want to be a cooper like his father. He wanted to be a doctor. This was his chance. His family had made sacrifices for him to have this opportunity — and would make more. Andrew's father planned to sell ten acres of family-owned land to pay for his tuition at Harvard. It was land they needed for trees to support the coopering business. "This dinner is about Harvard College, not Governor Wentworth!"

Joseph fumed. "Wentworth is an enemy of this community! I don't see why Dr. Cutter would invite him to his home."

Andrew shut his eyes tight. Enemy. That was the word that had been used as a branding iron against the royal governor. Andrew struggled to control his rising anger. "You know why. Governor Wentworth attended Harvard with Dr. Cutter. They're friends. Dr. Cutter moved to Portsmouth after college because he became friends with students from here. Governor Wentworth was one of them."

Joseph was unmoved.

Anger getting the better of him, Andrew fought to keep from being pulled further into what he knew was a losing argument. Joseph would not accept any alliance with the province's royal governor.

Despite the freezing temperature, Andrew felt a wave of heat pour over him. He was frustrated with Joseph, but he was also upset with the governor. Governor Wentworth had recently given many people, including Andrew, reason to doubt his loyalty to the citizens of New Hampshire. Governor Wentworth had helped General Gage — the governor of Massachusetts. But, in Andrew's mind, it was only doubt.

In Joseph's mind, Governor Wentworth was certainly an enemy, and Joseph was not alone in this belief. The Committee of Forty-Five had declared the governor an enemy, and publication of the committee's declaration in *The New Hampshire Gazette,* for all to read, had made it official. The article didn't mention the governor by name, but everyone knew it referred to Wentworth.

Andrew took a deep breath. "I just want to have dinner and talk about Harvard College."

Joseph's head shook from side to side. "You can't be friends with the enemy and Wentworth is our enemy. Think about it! Not only did he help Gage, Wentworth shut down the assembly just because he didn't like what was being discussed."

Andrew couldn't argue with Joseph's statement. On more than one occasion the governor dissolved the elected assembly. One of those times the assembly decided to meet, anyway, in the House Chamber. Governor Wentworth arrived with Sheriff John Parker and ordered the members to disperse — calling the meeting illegal. The men left peacefully but then went to a tavern to conduct their business.

"Everything is changing, Drew. You can't pretend it isn't. The British government keeps imposing taxes and trade restrictions. We have no say in Parliament. That's not right. We are British citizens."

His voice grew louder, "And if we don't obey, they'll try to crush us just as they did in Boston. Gage closed the port and stole the provincial gunpowder leaving the people in Boston defenseless against the King's troops. Boston is just the beginning — and you know it! We could be next, and Wentworth will help the British government against us."

Andrew was silent. As much as he didn't want to admit that things were changing, he knew they were. There had been boycotts and protests about policies in the past, but those were disagreements regarding policies that people expected would be peacefully resolved. Now, after the severe response to the tea incident, people were becoming nervous about how far the royal government would go to enforce its policies. People felt threatened.

Joseph and Andrew stood in the street — eye to eye. Joseph said, "You're going to have to decide which side you're on. Things are going to get bad now that we have agreed to follow the boycott. Parliament will close our port, just like they did in Boston. You wait and see. Your family depends on shipping too!"

Joseph deliberately bumped Andrew's arm as he pushed past him, leaving Andrew standing in the street, alone.

PORTSMOUTH PARADE
12:15 P.M.

☙ ☙ ☙

Jack Cochran hurried down King Street toward the center of town known as the Parade. A northeast wind had picked up and the clouds were thickening. He walked faster.

Jack's father had sent word to him at his grandparents' house to pick up documents from Governor Wentworth at the State House before taking the barge home to the fort. Along with collecting the documents, his mother had instructed him to purchase blue ribbons for his sister's upcoming birthday. Sally, the older of his two sisters, would soon turn ten.

He hurried down the street, needing to complete his errands and arrive at the barge in time for the tide to carry him home. On any spring, summer or fall day, he would have enjoyed traveling to the fort — but not today.

Although he looked forward to seeing his paternal grandfather, he wished he did not have to return to the fort during the week. His mother's parents had a very comfortable house in Portsmouth that

Jack appreciated, especially in winter. The family dwelling at the fort was not so comfortable. Rain often seeped in through the holes in the roof and the wind whistled through the walls during storms.

He tightened his hold around the collar of his wool coat with one hand as the wind cut through the flimsy material. In the other hand, he gripped the book Major Hale had given him to read over the next few days. He had taken the book, promising to study it carefully. But it was hard to imagine comprehending Virgil with a younger brother and two younger sisters running about their small dwelling. In this cold, they wouldn't be allowed to play outside, except for short periods of time.

But, Major Hale had insisted.

Jack neared the State House on the Parade. The fragrant aroma of roast pork arose from Tilton's Tavern. The smell of food always seemed stronger when the weather was cold. His stomach rumbled.

People darted in and out of shops. He caught sight of Primus Fowle, his hunched figure distinctive. Primus, a slave, worked for Daniel Fowle's newspaper, *The New Hampshire Gazette*. Primus was unable to straighten to full height from years of operating the printing press. Jack couldn't help but wonder how Primus felt working a printing press that allowed so many to share their thoughts with others through the written word, though he was never taught to read those words.

As Primus turned the corner, Jack gazed down the main street and saw John Wentworth, the province's young royal governor, descending the steps of the State House. Governor Wentworth looked up when he reached the street and saw Jack. He waved, gesturing for

Jack to join him. Jack picked up his pace, not wanting to keep the governor waiting.

The State House, a large wood structure with stone steps at the side entrances and a balcony on the second story, was an impressive building. It stood prominently in Portsmouth's town center. Complete with a large cupola and a roof balustrade, it served as the official offices for the capital of New Hampshire.

"Hello Jack." The governor's blue eyes sparkled. His warm hand shook Jack's half frozen one. The governor was a friendly man, in his thirties, handsome, and small in stature.

"I wasn't certain when you'd arrive, so I left the papers for your father inside," the governor said. "I'm about to go home to get my wife. Then we will have dinner at a friend's house."

Jack explained, "I'm a bit early. Major Hale ended the session before the normal time."

The governor's eyes narrowed and bore through Jack's. "Why? What has happened?" Even the governor knew it was unusual for studies at the Latin Grammar School to be interrupted.

Jack had already decided, as he walked to the State House, that he would tell the governor about the event at the wharf. He felt it was his duty. His father would have alerted the governor about a possible problem had he known about it.

"The Committee of Forty-Five was called out to stop Captain Chivers from loading fifty sheep onto his ship bound for the West Indies."

The governor exhaled slowly, his warm breath visible in the cold air. Jack searched his face. He expected anger, but saw none.

With a half-smile, Governor Wentworth said, "I have no doubt that some men take these actions with only the best intentions. But, I also have no doubt that many take these actions with only self-serving intentions."

Governor Wentworth looked out over the street as he spoke, "Some of the committee's actions have been petty. I actually rescued a shipment, keeping it from falling into the hands of the committee."

His smile was suddenly mischievous. He leaned toward Jack, sharing a small victory, "Three barrels of pineapples and oranges for General Gage's wife were on board a ship bound for Boston from the West Indies. When the ship stopped here, the committee wanted to confiscate the shipment. I had the barrels taken to my house for safe keeping and arranged for transport to Mrs. Gage over land."

Jack smiled, too. He was amused by both the story and the governor's unmasked glee.

Governor Wentworth added, "But come. Follow me. We'll get the documents together. It will give us a chance to talk for a few minutes."

A gust blew down on them. The governor started up the stairs and muttered, "And it will get us out of this wind." He passed through the doorway, holding the door open for Jack as he said, "I hope we don't have another Siberian winter. You could have walked home to the Castle that year."

Jack laughed. It was true. The mighty Piscataqua River froze that year and was passable on foot from Portsmouth out to Great Island where the fort was located.

"Yes, Sir. That was a remarkable year."

The governor closed the door securely as he shivered. "Let's hope it remains remarkable and not commonplace."

The street level of the State House was barren except for very large support columns. A wide staircase dominated the center of the first floor, ascending to the grand upper level.

Like all state houses in New England, the upper floor contained a large chamber in the middle for the elected representatives, as well as a courtroom and council chamber on either side.

They climbed the wide stairway together. Jack followed the governor into an office at the top. It was the governor's council chamber. A large wooden table and several chairs stood in the middle of the room and a smaller desk, strewn with writing supplies, was set against a wall. Embers in the fireplace glowed and the smell of burned wood was in the air.

The governor walked over to the desk and reached for the documents.

Though he was still young, Wentworth had been the royal governor for nearly seven years. Jack didn't live at the fort when the governor was inaugurated, but he lived in Portsmouth and remembered the gun salute at the fort in the governor's honor.

That had been a different time, quieter — more congenial. Now there was tension. But Jack had no doubts about the governor despite what some said about his loyalty to the people. Governor Wentworth was born and bred in Portsmouth. He was one of them — a New Hampshire man — just like Jack's father and the soldiers at the fort.

Jack's father said the governor had taken the right action in November, the action that upset some. His father said the governor had to help General Gage keep order in the neighboring province of

Massachusetts. He said the government was responsible for keeping the people safe.

Governor Wentworth turned to Jack with the document in his hand. "I was surprised to hear that you would collect this for your father today. In this weather, I hoped you were staying in town with your mother's family."

"I'm going back to the Castle tonight because my grandfather is coming from Londonderry for a visit."

"Oh! Wonderful!" The governor seemed genuinely pleased. "You'll have to give James my best. I'm sure your father will be very happy to see him. I know it's difficult being away from his family, but we so value your father's leadership at the fort."

Jack nodded. "Thank you, Your Excellency."

Jack was proud of his father's position as captain of His Majesty's Castle William and Mary. He had taken over the fort about three years earlier — in 1771. It had worked out well for Jack. Living in the Portsmouth area had allowed him to study with Major Hale.

Glancing at the book in Jack's hand the governor asked, "How are your studies coming along?"

"Quite well, Sir, except for some of the extra readings from Major Hale." As soon as the words were uttered, he wished he could take them back. He didn't want to sound as if he was complaining — to the governor.

Governor Wentworth's eyes narrowed. "Hopefully, he's not filling your head with nonsense about Parliament acting unconstitutionally."

"No, Sir," Jack said. "Absolutely not."

Jack was not surprised by the question. Major Hale's role in the

Committee of Forty-Five made some suspect that he tried to sway his students, but Major Hale did not try to influence his students in any way. Politics did not intrude into the schoolroom.

"Good." The governor seemed satisfied. "Well, I must be off to the Hut. I must not keep Mrs. Wentworth waiting."

Jack swallowed a smile. Governor Wentworth often referred to his home, rented by the province for his use, as the Hut. To Jack it was a very nice home, particularly compared to the drafty, plain dwelling that housed his family at the fort.

But the governor was accustomed to elegance. His family was quite wealthy. He had complained to the assembly, on more than one occasion, that his home was not up to what he believed was an appropriate abode for a governor of a province. So far the assembly had not agreed with him.

Jack and Governor Wentworth left the office and descended the stairs.

"Is Mrs. Wentworth feeling well?" Jack asked. He'd heard that Mrs. Wentworth was due to give birth to their first child very soon.

Governor Wentworth nodded proudly. "Quite well. Thank you for asking. I'll give her your best wishes."

On the street, a sudden gust whipped around the building and both Jack and the governor tightened their coats.

"I suggest you head quickly to the fort and a nice warm fire," he urged, reaching into his pocket and producing some coins. "But first, please go buy some maple candy for your brother and sisters."

Governor Wentworth often gave coins to children so they could buy candy and Jack would have been disappointed if he hadn't offered.

The governor winked as he added, "Perhaps there is enough for some candy for you, too."

"Thank you and good day, Sir."

"Good day, Jack. Please give my regards to your lovely mother. And tell your father that I will meet with him soon regarding another attempt to add more soldiers at the Castle."

Gripping the front of his coat, the governor hurried toward the Hut.

HOME OF DR. AMMI RUHAMAH CUTTER

2:00 P.M.

♛ ♛ ♛

Andrew slid his calloused finger across the nameplate by the front door, Dr. Ammi Ruhamah Cutter. Straightening his shoulders, he smoothed his hair with both hands then knocked.

Entering the parlor, Charles snickered as he eyed Andrew up and down. Andrew wore his finest breeches and new linen shirt. His shoes shone. He shot Charles a hard look.

"Andrew." Dr. Cutter rose from his chair. "You're right on time." He stepped forward and extended his hand. The doctor's comforting smile quelled Andrew's nervousness — at least for the moment.

"I'm sure you know our other guests." Dr. Cutter gestured to the governor and his wife.

"Yes, Sir," Andrew replied. His voice was tight and he hoped no one noticed.

Governor Wentworth stood and stepped toward Andrew. Smartly attired, as always, he had a charm about him and seemed to know it. He reached out warmly. "It's very nice that you could join us." His

41

grip was strong, but not overpowering, his gaze steady.

Andrew met his handshake with a firm grasp. He kept his eyes on the governor as he spoke, "Thank you. It is my privilege, Your Excellency." Andrew then bowed slightly to the governor's wife, a very attractive woman with long dark hair pulled up on top of her head as he said, "Mrs. Wentworth."

Andrew looked back at the governor's friendly face and felt that now familiar stab of betrayal sear through him. It physically hurt. This feeling had plagued him since November, just about a month before, when the committee declared the governor an enemy of the province. An enemy. Joseph's face flashed into his mind.

Andrew had just turned seven years old when John Wentworth became the Royal Governor of the Province, but his memories of the occasion were clear. It was the most exciting event he had ever witnessed.

The festivities to mark the occasion were lavish. A regiment of the local militia paraded and saluted as Mr. Wentworth ascended the steps of the State House. The High Sheriff publicly read the commission appointing him Governor and Commander in Chief of the Province. There was entertainment that lasted hours. But now, this same governor was considered an enemy.

Andrew stepped back and turned to Mrs. Cutter and Hannah who were seated. He half-bowed awkwardly toward them as Hannah smiled. Andrew was happy to smile in return. Hannah, the Cutter's fourteen-year-old daughter, looked beautiful. Her light brown hair was pulled up and tied with a silk ribbon that matched her dark green dress. Andrew was sure the deep color set off her clear green eyes

— even though he was too far away to be certain.

Hannah's older sister Mary stood near Charles. Older than Hannah by one year, Mary was quiet, serious and interested in matters of the home. Hannah, in contrast, was interested in politics, and Andrew knew she adored the royal governor.

Elizabeth, twelve, was seated next to Mrs. Wentworth, holding her hand. Elizabeth smiled shyly at Andrew as she told him, "We were just about to hear the names for the baby."

Andrew moved to the side — out of the way. A fire burned in the paneled fireplace. Above was a painting of a woman he didn't recognize. Decorative wainscoting surrounded the room. The home was far more elegant than the one he shared with his family just a few blocks away.

Mrs. Wentworth, now the center of attention, spoke, "We wish to name the baby after our dear friends in England, Lord and Lady Rockingham. So if it is a boy we will name him Charles, and if it is a girl, we will name her Mary." She smiled at Charles and Mary Cutter.

Mary brightened. She was clearly pleased.

Governor Wentworth sipped from a glass as he explained, "Lord Rockingham and I became close friends while I was in England on family business. That was before I was appointed governor. Lord Rockingham was instrumental in the repeal of the Stamp Act."

Andrew was familiar with the Stamp Act even though it had been enacted when he was only five years old. The Stamp Act required the use of stamps, or stamped paper, for many common needs such as newspapers, pamphlets and playing cards. Britain instituted the tax to raise revenue to pay off debts incurred by the war with France, and to pay for the troops that now remained in America. Some claimed the Stamp Act was the beginning of the problems between Britain and the colonies.

Pride swept over the governor's face as he spoke, "I assisted him in presenting the colonial point of view. I like to believe that helped to convince Parliament to change course." The look of pride now turned to one of concern. "Things would be different if Lord Rockingham was still in power."

"You supported repealing the Stamp Act?" Hannah asked. "I thought you would agree with all policy that comes from England."

The governor smiled slyly at her. "Does that surprise you?"

"Yes it does!" Her gaze was questioning, but not challenging.

He told her, "I thought it was a terrible policy. In fact, I emphasized to Lord Rockingham that the colonies' greatest value is trade. Anything that interferes with trade, including unreasonable restrictions and taxes, is harmful. Had the policy not changed, I may not have accepted the appointment as governor. It is difficult to uphold policies that you do not believe are correct. But, as an appointed official, I must."

"Do you think the British policies are correct, now?" Hannah leaned forward in her seat, engaging the governor.

He shook his head. "The only chance for harmony and a lasting relationship between Great Britain and the colonies must be built on mutual agreement and common advantage. The most effective way to accomplish this is to limit the restrictions on trade, not add to them. The current policy is very short sighted."

"Then why are you helping the British government enforce the policies?" Charles asked loudly from across the room. "Why did you recruit carpenters to build barracks for General Gage's soldiers? People say you are our enemy."

"Charles!" Dr. Cutter's tone was sharp as he shot his son a warning. "Governor Wentworth is a guest in our home."

Charles, confident as ever, simply shrugged. "I'm just asking. I didn't say I thought he is our enemy. I said people say that."

With a wave of his hand, Governor Wentworth defused the moment, "It is fine Ammi. I'm happy to answer his question."

Andrew's full attention was on the governor. This is the question he wanted answered, the question that had gnawed at him. Why had Governor Wentworth helped the unpopular governor of Massachusetts, General Thomas Gage?

During the previous fall, Gage had requested carpenters from New Hampshire to build barracks when none from Massachusetts would assist. Governor Wentworth contacted a friend in Wolfeboro, in the lakes region of New Hampshire, to recruit them and send them to Boston. But he supposedly did not tell them the purpose. When the Committee of Forty-Five found out, they were outraged. That's when they placed a notice in *The New Hampshire Gazette* proclaiming the governor an enemy to the community.

Andrew stepped closer as he waited to hear the governor's response.

Governor Wentworth set his glass down. "As a Crown official it is my duty to assist other governors in times of distress. I am bound by a Royal Instruction to render assistance. But most of all, it is my duty to maintain order. Order is the only way change can be effected without descending into chaos. With winter coming, and inadequate housing for the soldiers, they would have been quartered in private unoccupied buildings. Can you imagine the outrage in Boston if that occurred? The simple presence of soldiers in Boston is already an explosive situation."

He looked around the room with a bewildered expression on his face and added, "I thought people would agree that assisting was the right action to take."

"The soldiers should never have been brought to Boston in the first place," Dr. Cutter said.

"I don't disagree," the governor noted. "Their presence has made matters much worse."

"Everything the government has done recently has made matters worse," Dr. Cutter continued, "They don't understand the colonies at all."

Mrs. Cutter suddenly stood up. "Please, enough politics." The frown on her face was unmasked. Mrs. Cutter looked at her husband. "Ammi, didn't you wish to speak to Andrew about Harvard?"

The doctor smiled at his wife. "Yes, of course. This is why we invited Andrew to join us."

The doctor spoke to the Wentworths, "Major Hale has recommended that Andrew take the entrance exam for Harvard College this summer."

All eyes shifted to Andrew.

"How wonderful for you, Andrew," Mrs. Wentworth said.

Dr. Cutter turned to him. "Andrew, you will receive an excellent education at Harvard College. The emphasis is on classical languages,

Latin and Greek. But you will also study math, theology, logic and ethics, as well as natural philosophy ranging from physics and chemistry to astronomy."

Dr. Cutter added, "One of my fondest memories was standing on the roof of Old Harvard Hall gazing at Jupiter through Professor Winthrop's telescope."

"Jupiter?" Charles asked wide-eyed.

His father nodded. "You'll make some good friends too."

Charles spoke up "Maybe Andrew can make friends with someone other than Joseph Reed."

"Oh, Charles!" his mother chided. "This is a difficult time for the Reed family — for a lot of families."

Governor Wentworth said, "You will meet some remarkable people. I consider Ammi to be one of my closest friends." Governor Wentworth leaned back in the chair as he recalled, "My first year I roomed with a senior from Newport, Rhode Island. Andrew Malbone was his name. He was a lover of literature. From him I learned to appreciate some of the fine works of Swift and Pope."

Governor Wentworth suddenly turned his head to Andrew. "Are you familiar with Swift or Pope? You should be reading widely — not just Latin and Greek."

Andrew looked at a beaming Hannah. "Actually, Hannah introduced me to Alexander Pope. She loaned me a book of his poems."

Hannah's eyes glowed warmly in the afternoon light. "Did you select a favorite poem?" she asked.

Andrew suddenly felt hot. It was bad enough that Hannah held high expectations. He could see the hope in her eyes. But he hadn't anticipated Governor Wentworth to be knowledgeable about Alexander Pope.

"Andrew," Charles grinned as he spoke, "Did you select a favorite? Perhaps you can recite some of it for us."

Andrew shot Charles a hot glare.

"Oh yes! Please recite for us before we retire to the dining room," Mrs. Cutter requested. "I do so love to hear poetry."

Andrew's heart pounded. He placed his hand on the back of a chair and shot a grinning Charles another glare.

He looked at Hannah. "I particularly liked 'Ode to Solitude'."

"Oh, that is a beautiful poem," Hannah said, eyes sparkling.

"Oh yes, it is one of my favorites. Please recite some of it," Charles managed to say before he giggled.

Andrew's skin burned. He had practiced reciting the poem at home several times thinking he would recite it for Hannah, but suddenly he could not remember a word. He looked at her and she, perhaps aware of his distress, smiled at him. He took a deep breath and cleared his throat too loudly. Fortunately, the words came to him.

Happy the man, whose wish and care
A few paternal acres bound
Content to breathe his native air,
In his own ground.

"That's very nice, Andrew," Governor Wentworth praised. "It reminds me of the peace I feel up at our summer home in Wolfeboro."

"Yes." Mrs. Cutter agreed.

The Cutters and the Wentworths owned property in Wolfeboro, a beautiful area inland and to the north. Andrew had never seen it, but Hannah had told him about the large lakes. She said it was the most beautiful place she had ever seen.

Mrs. Wentworth tilted her head toward her husband. "John loves it so much he would like to spend more time there. But I am not the best traveler. He is a wonderful horseman and could ride right over the treetops if necessary. But for me it is quite a journey." Smiling she added, "Even when I am not in such a condition."

"Nonsense dear." The governor said with obvious affection for his wife.

"Andrew, why did you select that particular poem?" Dr. Cutter asked.

Suddenly relaxed Andrew answered, "Because it was one of the few I understood. Poetry is harder to understand than Latin."

Before he could regret his honesty, the room warmed with spontaneous laughter.

HOME OF DR. AMMI RUHAMAH CUTTER

3:45 P.M.

🐚 🐚 🐚

"Thank you, as always, for a lovely dinner." Mrs. Wentworth leaned forward and kissed Mrs. Cutter's cheek. Everyone was crowded into the narrow entryway by the stairs. Andrew and the Wentworths struggled with coats and capes.

Governor Wentworth fussed over his wife. "Dear, are you sure you don't want the carriage to take you home?" He stepped outside and frowned. "It is starting to snow."

Mrs. Wentworth shook her head. She was adamant. "I think the walk will be good for me."

The governor's eyes narrowed as he pursed his lips. Turning to Dr. Cutter he asked, "Ammi, is this wise?"

Dr. Cutter stepped outside and looked up at the gently falling snow. He patted his friend's shoulder. "If she wants to walk, she should walk."

The governor eyed the doctor with mild irritation.

Hannah volunteered, "Andrew and I will see them home." She

reached for her cape.

Warm from the heat in the house and hot food, the brisk air was welcome as they walked toward the Wentworths' home — the Hut — close to South Mill Pond. The snow fell gently and melted as it hit the ground.

"Hannah," Mrs. Wentworth said, "I have several books of poetry if you would like to borrow some of them."

"Thank you! Yes! That would be very nice."

"When we get to the house we'll pick something out," Mrs. Wentworth said, tightening her hold on her cape.

Governor Wentworth asked, " So Andrew, how are you preparing for the entrance exam this summer?"

"Tully and Virgil take up most of my time."

"Good. You will be required to prove your competence in Latin and Greek during your entrance exams."

The dull ache hit the pit of Andrew's stomach as he thought of all he needed to learn before summer. The process was intimidating. The exams were scheduled for the first Friday and Saturday in July and conducted by the tutors and the president of the college. "I am a bit nervous," he admitted.

Governor Wentworth had a gentle expression on his face. "I recall a friend, John Adams, had a fearful moment during exams. According to John, he was handed a passage to translate into Latin and saw words that he didn't recognize. As you can imagine, he broke into a sweat and watched his entire future disappear."

"John Adams? The lawyer from Boston?" It was Hannah who asked. John Adams was well known as a fine lawyer, but one who supported the Sons of Liberty, a group strongly opposed to recent royal policy.

The governor nodded. "Yes, that John Adams. But one of the tutors allowed John to use his study. On the desk was a Latin dictionary. The tutor told him to take all the time he needed."

Andrew exhaled a sigh of relief.

Hannah, never shy, asked, "Do you really think of John Adams as a friend?"

"Yes, I do," the governor replied without hesitation. "And I believe we want the same things — our rights as British subjects preserved. But, I do acknowledge that we disagree about how to achieve our common goal."

Mrs. Wentworth had taken hold of her husband's arm as they walked.

Sadness suddenly aged the governor's face beyond his years. "When I was in England during the Stamp Act controversy, the most troubling issue for Parliament, as well as the people on the streets, was the violence in the colonies. Thankfully the people of New Hampshire are, for the most part, reasonable and not prone to rash behavior."

The foursome stopped in front of the governor and Mrs. Wentworth's home, a large, white clapboard house. He told Hannah and Andrew, "If we wish to negotiate change, we must do it peacefully. Violence will be met with overwhelming force by the British government." Lines seemed to deepen in his face. "There is no doubt Great Britain can subdue the violence and subordinate the citizens here, but disgusted subjects will be useless." He looked down the street toward the Parade. "Perhaps dangerous."

Andrew stepped out of the small store in the Parade. He had just purchased maple candy. Eating one piece, he put the rest in his pocket. He had walked Hannah home after she and Mrs. Wentworth selected a book of poems for her to borrow. Governor Wentworth offered to loan Andrew a book called *Don Quixote*, which he took willingly. Andrew had no idea what it was about, but the governor assured him it was very entertaining and a good break from Tully and Virgil.

Andrew now looked down the street and saw a horse and rider approaching. Even at this distance, he could see this was not a casual visitor. Despite the frozen and rutted ground, the rider's head was down and the gray saddle horse moved with purpose.

Andrew watched as the horse and rider drew closer, heading toward the town center. Just down the street stood William Torrey. Well named, he was a Tory — a Loyalist. Very vocal about his support of royal policy, he angered many in the town. The approaching rider had caught his eye, too.

Andrew moved closer, determined to get a better look.

The rider reined in his horse, stopping next to William Torrey.

He did not look familiar to Andrew. He was a stocky man with dark hair visible from under his tricorn, with even darker eyes. Andrew couldn't help but observe the man's powerful wrists. But what commanded Andrew's attention was the grim expression on the rider's face — and the unmistakable urgency in his voice.

"I'm looking for Mr. Samuel Cutts." The rider said to Mr. Torrey, while the horse continued to move in an agitated manner, still full of energy. The rider held the reins tightly as he stated the purpose of his mission, "I have a very important communiqué to deliver to him."

Andrew knew the man the rider sought. Samuel Cutts was a member of the committee of correspondence.

"Again, can you tell me where I might find Mr. Cutts?"

Then Andrew saw it. A silver medal on the rider's jacket embossed with what he knew was a Liberty Tree. Under the tree were the words: Sons of Liberty.

He heard Mr. Torrey answer, "Sam Cutts is inside the tavern owned by Mr. Stoodley, just across the way." He pointed toward the garrison building across the street. "I just saw him go inside."

A look of relief washed across the rider's face.

The man dismounted and led the horse to Frank who had hurried out of the tavern when he saw the horseman arrive. Frank was one of Mr. Stoodley's slaves. He led the horse to the stable behind the tavern as the man with the important message entered the front door.

Andrew asked, "Excuse me, Sir. Who is that man who rode in on horseback?"

Mr. Torrey kept his eyes on the tavern and said, "Mr. Paul Revere from Boston."

"Paul Revere?"

Paul Revere, a talented silversmith and engraver, was known to be a very active member of the Sons of Liberty in Boston. He had carried messages to other colonies. Andrew's stomach tightened as he wondered what message he had brought. Paul Revere would not ride over sixty miles from Boston to Portsmouth unless it was urgent.

NEW CASTLE, PROVINCE OF NEW HAMPSHIRE
HIS MAJESTY'S CASTLE WILLIAM AND MARY
4:20 P.M.

♛ ♛ ♛

Jack had no sooner stepped off the barge, when in the dimming light of day, he saw his six-year old brother William running toward him. Coat wide open and hatless with silky blond hair blowing, William was full of energy.

"Jack! Jack!" he shouted.

He ran directly at Jack laughing, veering off as Jack reached out to him. He doubled back. "Ben told me you were coming!"

He took Jack's hand with both of his. William's hands were warm. He hadn't been outside long.

"I've been waiting for you. Did you bring anything?"

Jack ignored the question. "I hope you didn't pester Ben while he was on duty."

"I only asked him a couple of times if he could see the barge coming."

"Only a couple?"

William grinned.

His Majesty's Castle William and Mary stood on Great Island in the town of New Castle. It was strategically positioned to protect the town of Portsmouth, the provincial capital and major seaport for the colony.

The Castle, a term used for any fortified structure, was equipped with cannon, as well as muskets and gunpowder, some in storage awaiting deployment for naval or army use. All was stored safely in the most protected part of the fort under the watchful eyes of Jack's father and the soldiers stationed at the Castle.

Jack's father and the soldiers were part of the provincial militia. All militia served under the authority of Royal Governor Wentworth. The only difference between other militia soldiers and those at the fort was that the soldiers at the fort were paid, served full time and received uniforms and billeting.

"Welcome home, Jack." Ephraim nodded to Jack as he, and fellow soldier Isaac, hurried past Jack and William on their way to get the supplies that had crossed with Jack on the barge.

Ephraim Hall and Isaac Seveay, both New Hampshire men, had joined the fort during the past summer. They were able and trustworthy as were the other militia soldiers at the fort.

William, still grinning, pulled on Jack's free hand urging him to go faster. Pointing to Jack's other hand he asked, "Why do you have a book?"

"I only came home to see Grandfather. I can't fall behind in my studies, so I brought my studies with me."

William stopped pulling. He let go of Jack's hand. The grin was now replaced with a pout. "Oh," was all he managed.

"But," Jack reached down for William's hand. "We'll find time for fun."

William's bright smile returned.

"Has Grandfather arrived?" Jack asked his brother.

William shook his head. "No, but I have something to show you, Jack."

"Well then let's hurry!" Jack broke into a run, but kept a slow pace so William could keep up. At the last moment, Jack let William pass him as they reached the large gate to the fort.

Ben Rowell was standing guard duty and smiled at Jack and William as they ran through the open gate into Castle William and Mary. Samuel Rowell and John Griffiths were other soldiers who greeted them.

Jack and William hurried through the fort in the light snowfall to the family's living quarters. The fort's unremarkable interior was filled only with wooden barracks and a wooden house, along with two brick powder houses where the muskets and barrels of powder were stored. The house and barracks were small but livable, which was not the case when Jack's family moved there in early 1771.

Jack's father sought improvements upon arrival at the fort, even paying for some repairs and additions himself. The family dwelling and the soldier's barracks were in the poorest condition and had needed immediate attention. The chimney in the house was dangerously out of repair.

Fire had been the biggest concern. The powder house was located too close to the structures, particularly the barracks. Governor

Wentworth worked with the captain to obtain money from the assembly to make the fort and the structures safer.

"He's here!" Hurling the door open, William burst into the common room. Jack caught the door to quickly shut out the cold air. A welcoming fire burned in the large hearth in the central room.

Jack had barely closed the door before his sisters tripped over each other trying to get to him. "Let me remove my . . ." But the laughing girls came at him in all directions. Jack smiled as he handed the book, and the document for his father from Governor Wentworth, to his mother.

She shook her head in mild disapproval, but she couldn't subdue a smile as she watched the children with their outstretched hands.

She told Jack, "They have been waiting all afternoon for you to come home. Your father told them you were going to pick up a document from Governor Wentworth."

"Oh," Jack frowned, feigning sadness. "I didn't see the governor. He had already left before I arrived."

The children stopped in their tracks. Their faces fell, all excitement disappearing.

He looked at his smiling mother before cheering, "Yes I did!"

They children jumped up and down.

Jack enjoyed the attention for a few moments before he ordered, "Youngest first."

The loud groans came from Sally, nine, and Nancy, eight. But William beamed. His hand shot out and Jack dropped sweets into it. Jack thought of the little time he had for William these days.

"Me next!" Nancy spoke up. At eight, Nancy was not shy at all.

She definitely benefited from having two older siblings, particularly Sally who encouraged her sister. Nancy was confident, even bold. She shouted, "Thank you Governor Wentworth!"

Jack's mother laughed outloud. "And . . . ," she prompted her daughter.

"And, thank you Jack." Nancy curtsied, drawing more laughter.

Sally was last. Only a year apart, she and Nancy looked so much alike they could be twins. But Sally, whose real name was Sarah, after their mother, was the more serious of the two. Both studied hard. And while only boys could attend the Latin Grammar School, Major Hale provided lessons for girls during other times. Jack knew that Charles Cutter's sisters studied with him. Jack hoped one day his sisters would benefit from those lessons.

With candy in hand, the children drifted back to the table near the fire.

His mother gently hugged her son, whispering in his ear, "Did you remember the ribbons for Sally?"

"They are in my coat pocket," he whispered back.

She smiled, gave him another quick hug, and went back to the fire and hearth. Jack knew that later, when the children went to bed, his mother would search his pockets for the ribbons.

Mrs. Cochran stirred a pot in the center fire and Jack smelled molasses. No doubt the pot was full of beans cooking for their supper. He hoped it would include left-over ham from the family's dinner earlier in the day.

Jack hung his coat by the door and walked to the fireplace. He held his palms out until the heat was too much, then turned, his back to the fire.

William suddenly appeared before Jack, standing straight as a board. "Can you tell?" he asked.

Jack eyed his brother up and down.

His mother circled behind William, where he could not see her. She put her hand near his head.

Jack understood his mother's signal. Squinting one eye, he examined William even more closely. "Turn around, William," he said.

William turned obediently.

"Turn again."

William now faced Jack.

Jack said to his mother, who had returned to stirring the pot of beans, "I do believe, just in the few days I have been away, William has grown!"

William's grin stretched from ear to ear. "I have! Come and look at the measuring stick!" He grabbed Jack's hand. But before they left the room, the door opened.

Jack's father stomped his booted feet before entering the house.

Jack spoke to William, "You go ahead. I have to talk to Father."

William stomped his foot, and with a pout, left the room.

Captain Cochran pulled off his cloak and hung it by the door. "Isaac told me you had arrived." He moved to the fire, clapping one hand solidly on Jack's shoulder as he passed. "Did you bring the document from Governor Wentworth?"

Mrs. Cochran brought three steaming mugs to the table.

"Yes, Sir. It's on your desk. Governor Wentworth sends his regards to all and asked me to tell you that he is still working on getting more soldiers for the fort."

His mother muttered, "Try, as I know he will, it is a losing battle with this assembly. They will never vote for more soldiers."

Jack's father reached for a mug, but returned to the fire. "I know he'll try. But, the assembly still hasn't even voted to reimburse me for all of the money I spent on repairs."

"Hopefully the governor hasn't given up on pushing for your reimbursement," Mrs. Cochran said. "We certainly can't afford that cost."

"Nor should we," the captain agreed. "But I'm sure he will bring it up with the assembly again."

Mrs. Cochran looked less certain.

Pulling a chair out, Jack said, "There was some action at the wharf earlier today. The Committee of Forty-Five was called out."

"Major Hale, too?" Mrs. Cochran asked, shooting a glance at her husband.

His parents had both expressed concerns that Major Hale's political views may be influencing his students. From his earlier question to Jack, it was a concern that had obviously been shared by Governor Wentworth.

In addition to now being a member of the Committee of Forty-Five, Major Hale had served as moderator when the town passed the tea resolves condemning the Tea Act in December of the year before.

"Yes, he was called," Jack admitted, but quickly added, "he didn't say anything to us."

Mrs. Cochran pursed her lips then said, "He left the schoolroom. He left his students to attend to committee matters." It was a statement, not a question.

Jack cupped his hands around his mug and said nothing.

"So, why was the committee called out?" Captain Cochran walked to his desk and reached for the documents from the governor.

Jack quickly explained what had happened with Captain Chiver's shipment of sheep, but added that many had thought the shipment was tea.

"More tea shipments? Is that possible?" his mother asked.

"I don't think so," his father answered, "Especially now that an overall non-importation policy has taken effect. But, if Governor Wentworth becomes aware of any shipments, he will give me as much warning as possible."

In June, the mast ship, *Grosvenor* had entered the port with twenty-seven chests of East India tea bound for the merchant, Parry. Governor Wentworth had required Mr. Parry to send instructions to the ship's master through Captain Cochran. The tea was unloaded and carted to the Custom House before the town was even aware. Once it became known that the tea had been landed, a committee was formed to call on Mr. Parry and demand that the tea be re-shipped. He agreed and paid the duty. The tea was sent up north to Halifax within days.

In September, the mast ship *Fox* brought thirty chests of tea, again sent to Mr. Parry. After the attack on his house, Mr. Parry convinced representatives from the town that the tea had been shipped without his knowledge or approval. It was reshipped soon after he paid the duty.

Jack told them, "Charles Cutter said that no one would believe

Mr. Parry if it happened again."

"He is right about that," his father said. "The even tempers of the Portsmouth townspeople prevented the situation from getting too far out of hand both times, but I don't know if they would be able to do it again. People are becoming more agitated."

"Earlier today, Joseph Reed said he'd toss tea overboard if he had the chance," Jack said.

Mrs. Cochran sighed. "Well, if he or anyone in town does that we all should expect our port to close too."

"Some of the boys at school were talking the other day and said the British response to Boston's tea incident was too harsh."

"Harsh?" His mother countered. "What choice did Parliament have? Those men in Boston should never have thrown all that tea overboard. They destroyed valuable private property. The King and Parliament had to act."

Captain Cochran mused, "Twice, Governor Wentworth allowed the tea to be reshipped after the duty was paid. But the Portsmouth townspeople allowed Ed Parry to pay it. In Boston, some protesting townspeople wanted the tea reshipped *before* paying the duty."

Jack said, "I heard that Governor Hutchinson in Massachusetts did not allow it because his sons were the consignees and would lose money on the shipment."

His father nodded, taking a sip from his mug. "Yes, that's true, but I think there were other reasons. Governor Hutchinson had problems with the Sons of Liberty before."

"Sons of Violence, you mean." Mrs. Cochran spoke, contempt etched in her face, "But General Gage is governor now."

Captain Cochran looked from his wife to Jack. "Let's hope the problems in Boston don't work their way up here to New Hampshire."

Suddenly William appeared in the doorway. "Jack! Come look at the measuring stick!"

MR. STOODLEY'S TAVERN
4:45 P.M.

🐚 🐚 🐚

Andrew slid through the tavern door, closing it quickly to keep the frigid air outside. Two steps into the room, he wished for any fresh breeze inside the cramped entryway. Men spilled out of the common rooms. Some stood on the steps of the wide staircase. The air stank of smoke, ale, and men.

All eyes turned to meet his, followed by grumbles of displeasure. The men were anxiously waiting for someone and it wasn't Andrew. He knew they were waiting for committee members. Andrew stepped into the closest room just to get out of the way.

Immediately after Mr. Revere left the tavern, the call went out to the members of the committee of correspondence to meet at Mr. Stoodley's public house. Right after that, Mr. Torrey left the Parade likely headed to the home of Governor Wentworth to warn him about Mr. Revere's sudden visit.

A voice near Andrew asked loudly, "Are you sure John Langdon is on his way?"

"A message was sent to his house," someone answered.

Another voice jeered, "I hope the message wasn't left with his brother, Woodbury!"

Laughter laced with contempt rolled through the tavern. Some suspected that Woodbury Langdon was a Tory, but his positions regarding politics tended to shift, making it difficult to be certain.

Part of an established Portsmouth family, both Woodbury and John Langdon were wealthy merchants. John Langdon lived at his brother's house on Broad Street, but Woodbury and John could not have differed more. The joke around town was, despite the enormous house they shared, no house was large enough for two men with such opposing political viewpoints.

"Leave the front door open," a man holding a mug of ale said. "Maybe some of the air will make it in here!"

Four more men crowded into the already jammed room forcing Andrew further inside.

"Get some air in here!" the same man shouted, this time over the loud voices in the tavern. Someone else said, "Open a window."

Andrew stepped back close to the wall.

It was then that he saw Samuel Cutts, the man Paul Revere sought out regarding urgent news. Mr. Cutts, a merchant in the town who'd had a ship, the *Resolution*, seized by custom officers, sat on the far side of the room. His forearms rested on the table, his hands clasped tightly together. He stared into the room with a hollow expression that sent a chill down Andrew's spine.

Other members of the committee of correspondence sat silently at the table with him. To his right was the Honorable John Sherburne,

middle-aged and a moderate member of the governor's council. Also
at the table was Jacob Sheafe, a wealthy merchant in his sixties who,
like Samuel Cutts and other merchants, had prospered prior to the
restrictive policy measures. Rounding out the group was a local car-
penter and cabinet-maker, George Gains.

Andrew searched other faces in the tavern. Some were familiar,
but others were not. The men who filled the tavern were like those
who filled the town of Portsmouth, a blend of merchants and crafts-
men, some wealthy, some not, some who supported the actions taken
by the disguised men in Boston who threw tea into the harbor, and
some who did not.

Frank and Flora, Mr. Stoodley's slaves, hurried through the tavern setting down bowls of punch and plenty of mugs. Tavern owner
Mr. Stoodley, arms folded over his massive chest, stood watching.

A cold draft pressed into the room once more and all eyes darted
toward the common-room door. The disappointment was now tinged
with anger as Joseph stepped inside. Someone shouted, "Forget about
Langdon. You have enough committee members here."

A rumble of agreement swept through the over crowded room.

Another voice insisted, "Just tell us what this is about! Why was
the committee called together?"

There were more rumbles and this time Andrew joined in. The
secrecy surrounding the contents of the message delivered by Mr.
Revere made him nervous.

"We wait for John Langdon." Samuel Cutts was clear.

No man challenged him.

Joseph snaked his way through the crowded room toward Andrew.

"What's going on?" Joseph asked. "I heard that the committee of correspondence members were called to the tavern."

Andrew, keeping his voice low told Joseph, "A rider came into town late in the afternoon, I was there when he arrived." He whispered, "It was Paul Revere from Boston with a message for Mr. Cutts."

"Paul Revere?" Joseph's eyebrows arched, a thin smile crossed his lips.

Andrew eyed his friend's expression, silently wishing Joseph had not come to the tavern. This was likely the type of trouble he feared Joseph longed for and the type he hoped to avoid. Joseph reached through two seated men for a mug on the table and filled it with punch.

Joseph took a swig. Then, with a flash of suspicion in his eyes, asked, "Why didn't you find me and tell me?"

Before he could form an explanation that would satisfy Joseph, someone Andrew did not recognize turned and faced them.

"I hear it was Paul Revere too. Little good ever comes from that man. He stirs up trouble as easily as stirring up stew in the kitchen."

Joseph laughed as the man moved away from them. Andrew, on the other hand, was certain the man had not made the statement as a joke.

The door opened again and John Langdon stepped into the room. Silence fell over tavern.

Langdon was a strong, handsome man in his early thirties whose entry would quiet a room on any occasion. His eyes searched the crowded tavern. Unable to see the seated man, Mr. Langdon quickly demanded, "Where is Sam Cutts?"

A quiet voice said, "Over here, John." Cutts pressed his hands on the table and rose slowly, wearily, as if a weight bound him down. Men stepped aside to allow Langdon to pass.

When Langdon reached Samuel Cutts, the two men stood looking at one another for a moment. Then Cutts gestured toward the chair across from his, saying to the silent crowd, "We will take a moment."

Another grumble passed through the tavern, but subsided quickly.

John Langdon's presence gave Andrew a moment's relief. An accomplished man, Langdon was not a hot head. He would have a reasoned opinion about the news that Mr. Revere brought and the men would listen to him.

There was no doubt in Andrew's mind that Mr. Langdon was a supporter of the non-importation policy. And he had his own reason to dislike British policy. A ship that carried a cargo of sugar and rum for John Langdon had been seized and condemned by an admiralty judge. Despite a forceful appeal, Langdon lost all of his cargo.

The committee members at the table now leaned forward talking quietly but intently. Anxiety, frustration and the closeness in the room caused tempers to flare.

A man stood, his angry voice boomed. "Tell them now or I will!"

Sam Cutts rose heavily, glaring at the man who spoke. He then searched the room slowly making eye contact with one man, then another. His eyes met Andrew's. Rage tinged with fear reflected in Mr. Cutt's eyes.

No one spoke. No one lifted a mug of punch or ale. No one moved.

Mr. Cutts took a long slow breath and spoke, "Just past 4:00 this afternoon, a letter from William Cooper from the Boston Committee of Correspondence was delivered to me by Paul Revere."

The room was quiet.

He paused. Again, his eyes searched the room.

"The express letter informed us that gunpowder has been removed from the fort in Rhode Island and taken inland for safe-keeping."

A few utterances were heard, but most sat silently, likely wondering why the people in Rhode Island thought their powder was safer outside of the protection of the fort. Andrew was one of those who wondered. Something in Mr. Cutts' face conveyed there was more, and the room quieted quickly.

His voice even, Mr. Cutts told the men crowded into the tavern, "The express carried word that a Royal Order has been issued to prohibit the export of gunpowder to the colonies. And the governors have been ordered to prevent the import of arms."

Those in the room remained quiet. Andrew tried to make sense of the order. He thought the problems were only in Massachusetts. Why was the British government preventing other provinces from receiving powder and arms?

"They don't want us to be able to protect ourselves!" a man by a window shouted as if in answer to Andrew's question. "They don't want us to be able to protect ourselves from them!"

A thin, blond-haired man agreed, "The British government plans to shove their unfair policies down our throats, even attack us if we don't submit. We won't be able to stop them if we don't have powder and arms!"

Someone raged, "Never! We must never allow ourselves to be slaves!"

Flora dropped a pewter platter on a table from a considerable height. The clattering sound echoed around the room, but few took notice. Andrew watched her eyes dart to Frank who stood glaring at the man who made the remark. His anger-filled eyes met Flora's.

Andrew suddenly found it difficult to breathe.

From the back of the room someone yelled, "That is why Rhode Island moved the powder from the fort! They were afraid Gage would seize it for the British regulars — just like he did in Boston."

Jeers filled the room.

A man near Andrew agreed, "Gage will come after our powder, too! We won't be able to get more! We need a plan!"

Andrew sat frozen. He had been unnerved by the action taken by General Gage in September. During the night Gage's soldiers removed powder from the Provincial Powder House outside of Boston.

Joseph poked an elbow into Andrew's ribs. "I told you!"

Sam Cutts looked at John Langdon. A solemn Langdon nodded.

Mr. Cutts turned back to the men huddled inside the room. He took another deep breath before he spoke. Andrew, suddenly sweating, felt the closeness in the room. There was more.

Mr. Cutts said, "The express warned that British troops have boarded a ship in Boston."

The room was stone silent. All eyes were on Mr. Cutts.

He struggled as if what he was about to say was not possible. Andrew held his breath.

"It is believed that the British regulars are on their way here to

71

His Majesty's Castle William and Mary to seize our weapons and munitions and to take control of the fort."

Gasps roared through Mr. Stoodley's tavern. Andrew steadied himself, placing a hand on the table beside him.

Joseph pushed his irate face close to Andrew's. His breath was hot on Andrew's cheeks. "Gage! He is going to take our powder just like he did near Boston! And he is one of Wentworth's friends."

The room seemed to close in on Andrew. The air was thick and his head throbbed.

Joseph's eyes blazed. "So did your school friend Cochran tell you troops are on the way?" Joseph's breath smelled of punch. "What about Wentworth? Did he announce that British regulars were coming to take over our fort while you had dinner at the Cutter's house?"

Andrew had no answer. Was it possible that both Jack and the governor knew about General Gage's plan? Jack did go see the governor, and it was odd that Jack left school midweek to go back to the fort. Was the story about his grandfather visiting true? And what about Governor Wentworth? He did say the British government could subdue the people. Was that the plan? Did Dr. Cutter know? The room seemed to spin.

Joseph remained in Andrew's face. "Jack Cochran is probably getting the barracks ready for the King's troops right now! That's why he hurried home to the fort!"

Andrew had heard enough. With his forearm, he pushed Joseph away.

Joseph was back in his face in an instant. "Wentworth is not going to help us. Instead, he will help Gage destroy us."

Andrew knew the governor had to help General Gage if asked. He was bound by a Royal Instruction to take action.

"To the fort!" a shout rang out inside the crowded room.

"To the fort!" Joseph joined the call.

"To the fort!" A chant echoed through the packed tavern. "To the fort! To the fort! To the fort!" Men stepped forward, moving everyone with each step. Andrew's feet slid on the wood floor.

John Langdon leapt up. "Order!" he shouted out over the rising mob. "There will be order!"

"To the fort! To the fort!" they yelled.

Andrew braced against the men pushing.

"Order!" Scrambling up onto a chair, Langdon called out again, "Order!"

The crowd quieted. The forward movement stopped.

Langdon continued shouting, "We must have order! We will decide the proper action. Go home!"

"No! No! To the fort! To the fort!" they yelled.

"Go home for now!" Langdon roared above the crowd. "But be prepared to answer the call!"

HIS MAJESTY'S CASTLE WILLIAM AND MARY
11:00 P.M.

⚜ ⚜ ⚜

Jack stood motionless, gripping his musket. With every blast of icy air that swept over him, he unconsciously held his breath until each gust of wind subsided. One, two, three, four, five…he drew in a short breath, careful not to take in too much cold air at once.

He stepped into the guardhouse as he wondered, *Where's Ephraim?*

Under the strict orders of Governor Wentworth, the soldiers had been on watch since 6:00 in the evening after an express arrived at the fort. Jack read what it said, "Examine every person that comes into the Fort and be vigilant against all Force and Stratagem."

Jack wondered what that meant. Who would come to the fort and why should they be on guard? He stepped outside, again, and peered through the gate. The fort was protected by a six to eight-foot stone wall with seaward facing embrasures — window-sized openings for weapons. Any attack on the fort would normally come from the water. The fort was equipped with garrison cannons positioned along the fort walls and field cannons that could be moved.

The fortification had been repaired, but the bigger problem was the lack of soldiers.

When Jack's father arrived, in addition to seeking repairs, he asked Governor Wentworth for more soldiers, concerned the number of soldiers was insufficient for garrison duty. He also worried that soldiers would leave the fort after their duty ended due to low wages and poor billeting.

Of the five soldiers currently protecting His Majesty's Castle William and Mary — Isaac Seveay, Ephraim Hall, Benjamin Rowell, Samuel Rowell, and John Griffiths, Jack knew Isaac and Ephraim the best. He hoped they would remain at the fort.

Jack raised his eyes to the sky. Snow no longer fell, but the clouds had not cleared. Light from the forty-foot-tall lighthouse reflected off a thin layer of snow, allowing him to see out. Nothing had happened, at least so far. He exhaled loudly.

The fort was so undermanned that even his father would take a watch this night. The five soldiers and his father would stand watch for four hours each throughout the night and into the morning. Young Jack had volunteered for guard duty as well, but his father forbade it. Not yet sixteen, he wasn't old enough to be a militia member and his father always followed the rules.

However, Captain Cochran did agree to allow Jack to relieve the men for a few minutes to warm themselves in the barracks and get a hot drink. Ephraim was especially pleased to get a break.

At a different time, any soldier could have left his post for a few minutes. And in this frigid weather, the captain wouldn't have objected if a guard left long enough to play a game with dice as well. The soldiers had hammered musket balls into rough dice to pass the time. But not tonight.

"Examine every person that comes into the Fort and be vigilant against all Force and Stratagem." Those were the governor's exact words in the express.

Jack had repeated them in his head over and over and over. Who would use force? Who would strategize to take over the fort?

The soldiers were nervous. So was Jack. Such an order had never been issued directly from the royal governor. In fact, no similar order had ever been issued by anyone at any time. Captain Cochran, usually open with the men, had said little. And he hadn't told Jack anything more than he told the soldiers. Captain Cochran didn't have any more information to give. The governor had not told him why the unusual order was put in place.

Jack had eavesdropped on his parent's muffled conversation. That was how he knew his father had not just shielded him or the soldiers from information. Captain Cochran didn't know any more than what was stated in the order.

Jack peered through the slats of the front gate of the fort. The gate faced inland on the narrow neck of land on the island. The lighthouse threw shadows onto the ground. Nothing was out of the ordinary.

Jack still could not imagine why anyone would attack the fort. There had been some disagreements among people in Portsmouth about whether to assist the people of Boston and whether the current boycott was a good idea, but nothing about the fort had been discussed. The only disagreements about the fort were about funding, but that had already been debated and decided. No more soldiers — no more funding. But Jack recalled what happened in October of 1771. It had left him uneasy.

In that year, the brig, *Resolution*, owned by Samuel Cutts, entered the port and registered its cargo at the Piscataqua Customs House. Two days later the collector, believing the shipmaster had not reported molasses onboard, seized the ship and part of its cargo. To protect the ship and contents, Governor Wentworth had ordered Captain Cochran and four soldiers onboard. But at midnight fifty armed and disguised men and boys boarded the ship, overpowered the captain and soldiers, and took forty to fifty hogsheads of molasses.

There was a sudden snap of a twig. Jack immediately swung his musket into position, ready to fire if necessary. He gripped the weapon tightly. His eyes scanned outward, moving quickly from side to side. With so little light, it was impossible to be certain that no one lurked in the darkness. He heard another snap, but this time further away. He relaxed his grip, lowered the musket and looked back into the fort. No sign of Ephraim. Jack stepped back inside the guardhouse to escape the increasing wind. He stretched his numb fingers. The guardhouse didn't offer any real protection from the cold, but at least it kept some of the wind out.

Where's Ephraim?

ANDREW'S HOME
December 14, 1774
Noon

♛ ♛ ♛

Andrew pounded a hoop driver with a hammer, tightening the hoop that held a barrel together. He had promised his father that he would work on some of the barrels while his family was away.

The repetitive motion was somehow comforting. He was in control, something he had not felt since he left the tavern the evening before. He stopped long enough to wipe the sweat from his brow. Even though it was bitterly cold, the work kept him warm. He glanced outside and thought it close to noon. Perhaps the members had decided not to act on Mr. Revere's information. Perhaps they had received word that the news was not correct. He hoped the news was not correct.

Andrew set the barrel aside and took another.

He had barely slept. Many left the tavern following Mr. Langdon's plea to return home. Andrew wished he had too, but he stayed hoping to get more information. The committee members had retired to another room and the talk among the men who remained had become bolder as they drank. Joseph joined in the conversations as he moved from table to table.

Late in the evening, the talk turned to violently taking His Majesty's Castle, but only a few supported the idea. Andrew thought of Jack. In addition to Jack and his parents, Andrew knew he had younger siblings who lived at the fort. A violent attack would be dangerous for them.

He couldn't shake the doubt that had crept in about Jack. Did he know that regulars were on the way? And what about Governor Wentworth? The governor hadn't said anything during dinner with the Cutter family. But would he?

Andrew pounded the hoop driver — harder this time.

If the committee decided to act, Andrew was confident the plan would be well thought out. The members of the committee of correspondence were reasonable men, selected for that trait. They were the type of men Governor Wentworth described as typical of New Hampshire. They were not the men who talked of violence. Andrew was certain they would do their best to avoid it.

Violence is what the governor said was so upsetting to the Parliament and the people living in Britain. And people here said the British government was looking for an excuse to close the port. Violence would give them an excuse.

The powder was taken from the fort in Rhode Island without any violence, but Andrew learned, later in the evening, that the powder was taken by an official order. Rhode Island was governed differently than New Hampshire.

He pounded again. This hoop was more difficult.

A rumbling sound stopped him.

It sounded like thunder, but thunder was extremely rare in December. He sat perfectly still and listened. In the distance he now made out the distinct roll of drums followed by the shrill sound of fifes.

Andrew let the barrel fall. There was no mistaking it. An alarm had been sounded! It was a call to action. A decision had been made. He grabbed his wool coat and ran from his house toward the Parade.

Men and boys, even women and girls swarmed down the street toward the call of the fifes and drums. They all descended on the Parade within minutes. Everyone wanted to hear the decision.

Tall as Andrew was, it was difficult to see over the masses of men crowded together, many as out of breath as Andrew. One red-faced stranger to his right wore no coat even though snow was again falling. He likely had forgotten to put one on in his rush to the Parade.

Circling the crowd, Andrew pressed his way through just in time to see a number of men marching through the streets, drums beating. Surrounding them were at least one hundred other men.

The sheer number was intimidating, but the anger building in the crowd was frightening. Andrew felt himself being jostled as men pushed forward toward the fifes and drums.

John Langdon and Thomas Pickering led the march. Others shouted, pumping their arms into the air. Some men carried axes and crowbars, and menacingly waved them as the shouting grew louder.

Andrew's eyes were drawn to men exiting the State House. Governor Wentworth's private secretary, Thomas Macdonogh, and the Chief Justice and Secretary of the Province, Theodore Atkinson, Sr., ran down the steps toward the gathering mob.

Andrew lost sight of them as he was pushed deeper into the gang of angry men on the street. He feared he might be knocked off his feet and trampled. Then he heard a familiar voice. "What is the purpose of this gathering?" Chief Justice Atkinson called out above the shouting in the street.

The pushing stopped. Andrew stepped through an opening in the mass of bodies. He could now see the Chief Justice.

Atkinson demanded again, "What is the purpose of this gathering?" His voice was tight with apparent anger. An older man, he was used to receiving respect from others — not challenges. He stared at each man standing close to him.

Many men did not meet his gaze, looking away. Many stepped back from the man of authority. But no one answered the question.

The Chief Justice eyed the mob, again. Growing impatient, he said, "I believe you plan to attack King George's Fort!"

Still no one spoke, though some looked around uncomfortably.

Atkinson eyes blazed as he bellowed, "You plan to take the powder from the fort!"

No one denied the claim.

His anger rising, he told the crowd, "If you take powder from His Majesty's Fort, you will answer for this act of rebellion for twenty years! No! You will answer for as long as you live!"

Andrew's blood ran cold. Rebellion?

Murmurs came from the crowd as some agreed with the Chief Justice's words.

Many more now looked about uncomfortably. No longer were

they in the company of supporters like the night before in the tavern. This was the Chief Justice warning of the consequences of such an action. He was calling it rebellion.

John Langdon leapt to the steps. In a bold voice he implored, "We can no longer believe in this government! They are determined to crush us if we try to assert our rights as British citizens! We have seen it in Boston and we are next! British regulars are on the way! We must take what is ours! We must protect ourselves and we must protect our families! To the fort!"

"To the fort! To the fort!" Men rallied around Langdon as their new leader.

The mob spontaneously moved with purpose and Andrew with it. To resist would have been like trying to swim against the tide of the swift-flowing Piscataqua River. But Andrew didn't want to resist. The Chief Justice did not deny that the King's troops were on the way to take over the fort. The people were in danger. He had to act. There was no choice in his mind. He joined his neighbors who marched to the waterfront determined to protect the citizens of New Hampshire.

John Langdon shouted orders as men swarmed the water's edge. But it was impossible to hear him above the loud voices.

Someone yelled in Andrew's ear, "Load quickly!"

Small scows and flat-bottomed gundalows and barges bobbed in the water.

A young man, in his early twenties said, "I heard gundalows from Kittery are already on the way to the fort! Men from Rye are crossing the bridge over Little Harbor! Men are standing by in New Castle!"

It was then that Andrew realized this was a coordinated plan. It wasn't just men from Portsmouth inspired by Mr. Langdon's speech at the State House. This plan had been in the works. Messengers had been sent — probably during the night. Men from both sides of the Piscataqua River, men from New Hampshire and Massachusetts were rallying to the cause.

A hand grabbed Andrew's sleeve and pulled him through the throng of men gathered along the shoreline. It was Joseph. They weaved their way through the agitated group. Reaching a clearing, Andrew looked at Joseph. For the first time in months, Joseph looked happy. He released his grip on Andrew's sleeve and slung his arm over his friend's shoulder. "I knew you'd make the right choice. I knew you were with us. We're going to take what is ours!"

A large gundalow floated before them, loaded with close to thirty men packed on board. Another floated just yards away. Other small boats arrived to the cheers of men waiting to board them.

Gundalows were common in the Piscataqua region. Square ended and flat bottomed, these barges allowed travel in three or four feet of water. But right then, they looked unsteady as agitated men jumped aboard.

"Keep moving!" The men crowded close, stepping onto the barge quickly, methodically. Everyone knew time was critical if they were to catch the powerful ebb tide.

The Piscataqua River has one of the strongest tides in the world. Twice a day, the seven-foot tide pushed salt water inland into Little Bay and Great Bay. And twice it took the water back out again. Five freshwater rivers flow into the bays, stretching for miles inland. In a flood tide, a gundalow traveled the twenty-five miles from Portsmouth to the town of Exeter in a little over two hours.

"Ebb tide and an ash breeze is all we need. Hurry!" a man with a large hat, pulled low, cried out.

Andrew looked down at the long oars, called sweeps. They were made of ashwood. The men handling the oars would provide the necessary ash breeze.

Andrew was pushed toward the stern of the gundalow. "We've got to steady the barge. Move along!" a man directed.

Andrew's eyes darted from bow to stern. He saw Joseph was now about six feet from the bow of the gundalow.

The men squeezed in tighter and Andrew was jostled dangerously close to the edge. The frigid water lapped less than a foot away. He longed to be safely nestled in the middle of the gundalow away from the icy water and biting air.

A voice came from Andrew's right side. The man did not look familiar. "I heard that a few New Castle men are going to try to enter the Castle prior to our arrival."

"I heard the same," another unfamiliar man responded. "They are going to try to speak with Captain Cochran."

The other man said, "Cochran's one of us. He isn't a British military officer. He's from New Hampshire. He will help us. It will be easy — just like in Rhode Island."

Andrew hoped he was right.

HIS MAJESTY'S CASTLE WILLIAM AND MARY
2:00 P.M.

☙ ☙ ☙

Jack sat at the family table in the chair closest to the fireplace. Dinner simmered in a pot, but he had no appetite. He had tried to study, but found it impossible. The book lay unopened on the wooden table. In his hand he held the express from Governor Wentworth that had been delivered the previous evening. He read it again, but it wasn't necessary. He had memorized the words. "Examine every person who comes into the Fort, and be vigilant against all Force and Stratagem."

Jack dropped the express onto the table, frustrated by the message. Why hadn't the governor told them what to watch for?

His mother joined him. She smiled weakly. "Hopefully we will hear something soon." Jack saw the worry in her eyes.

Neither of his parents had said much about the express, not wanting to upset the younger children who now played in the next room having finished their lessons with their mother. She taught them at home because the school for younger children was a distance from the fort.

From the sound coming from the next room, Jack knew they were playing Knucklebones, a game that used small sheep bones. To play, one bone is selected to toss into the air and the player tries to pick up one bone from the floor before catching the tossed bone. If successful, the bone is tossed and two are picked up from the floor and so on. Jack had enjoyed the game when he was younger. He was glad the children were distracted.

The door swung open. Captain Cochran came in bringing a blast of cold air with him. Before he could close the door Jack asked, "Any word from the governor?"

Removing his coat and hat, his father shook his head. "No, but I still hope to receive word soon that the crisis is over since nothing happened last night."

It had been a long night. And it had been a long morning. They tried to maintain a normal schedule, but the children were kept inside the house as an extra precaution. The girls knew something was wrong, Jack was sure, but they didn't ask. William just pouted. He wanted to go outside.

There was a sharp knock at the door.

Jack's father called out, "Enter."

"Captain Cochran." Ephraim appeared in the doorway. "There are two men at the gate who wish to speak with you. They are local men, I recognize both of them, but I thought I should talk with you prior to allowing them inside the fort."

"Yes Private Hall, you were right to come to me first given the express from last night. You say they are local men. What are their names?"

"Stephen Batson and Henry Langmead, both from here in New Castle, Sir. They say they wish to speak with you about a business matter."

"Business?"

"Yes, Captain. That is what they said."

Jack's father nodded. "Perhaps they read in the *Gazette* that I received funding to hire a keeper for the lighthouse. Maybe one, or both, are interested in the job. I know the men, not well, but I know them to be from New Castle. It's cold outside. Send them in. I will speak with them."

"Yes Captain." Ephraim closed the door to the dwelling.

Captain Cochran remained on his feet, ready to greet the two visitors. Mrs. Cochran said, "I'll go check on the children." With a light laugh she added, "They have been far too quiet."

"Do you think these men may bring word from the governor?" Jack asked.

"No Jack, I don't. A Portsmouth man would deliver any express from Governor Wentworth, not men from New Castle. It's more likely they have come to apply for the job of lightkeeper. I hope one of them is suitable. It has been a burden on all of us tending that light ourselves."

Jack moved away from the table, but stood close to the fire, disappointed that the men were not likely to have been sent by Governor Wentworth. It would be another long day and night if the governor didn't send word soon that they could stand down. If the men did not bring word that the threat was over, he, too, was hopeful that the men had come to apply as lightkeeper. The soldiers, and sometimes Jack,

87

had tended the lighthouse since it was built in 1771.

Ephraim returned with two men, then left immediately to resume his post. The men wore heavy dark cloaks, hats drawn low and stood just inside the doorway.

Both looked at Jack first, nodding to him, then the two exchanged glances with each other. Captain Cochran shook hands with each of the men, greeting them by name and gestured toward the table and chairs. "Please remove your coats. Warm yourselves by the fire."

"Thank you, Captain. There is quite a wind outside," Stephen Batson spoke. He took a quick look around the room, his eyes stopping on Jack again.

The captain following his gaze said, "You know my son, Jack."

Batson and Langmead nodded acknowledging Jack one more time.

Batson said to him, "We didn't expect to see you here. Thought you'd be in town."

Jack didn't respond, surprised the men knew he stayed in town during the week for school.

The men moved closer to the fire, but did not remove their coats or hats. Nor did they sit down.

Jack watched Langmead as he looked around the room. His eyes darted right and left. He appeared nervous.

Captain Cochran asked, "What brings you men out on such a cold December day? My guard informs me that you have some business to conduct with me. Have you come to apply for the position of lighthouse keeper?"

"We—"

Langmead barely got a word out when Batson interrupted. "Yes. We heard you needed someone."

Langmead nodded. "That's what we heard."

"Good," Captain Cochran was visibly pleased. "It has been difficult on the soldiers to have that extra duty. The lighthouse is very important, but it takes up much of our time."

Batson said, "We also heard you might be getting some new soldiers here at the fort."

"No," the captain was clear. "Where did you hear that? I hope that wasn't reported in the *Gazette*. We need the soldiers, but we haven't received any funding."

"No," Batson told him. "It wasn't in the *Gazette*. Just heard."

Captain Cochran explained, "Governor Wentworth has had difficulty getting the assembly to agree to fund the cost of adding more men."

Batson sympathized. "Just doesn't seem right. When did you last make the request?"

"It was in March of this year that the request for more funding for soldiers was made. The assembly only saw fit to fund three soldiers and one officer. Governor Wentworth was appalled — as was I."

Jack glanced over and saw his mother standing in the doorway of the adjoining room. She was listening.

The captain continued, "After much effort on the governor's part, the assembly finally authorized five enlisted men and myself."

Langmead spoke, "I've been told you have plenty of cannons and muskets. And I hear you have fifty barrels of gunpowder."

The captain remarked, "More."

"Is the powder all in the powder houses we saw as we entered the gate?"

Before the captain could answer, the guard entered. "Captain, there are a few other men outside looking for Mr. Batson and Mr. Langmead. They are all New Castle men."

"Some of the neighbors heard about the lightkeeper position, too." Batson said quickly.

Jack was surprised so many were interested in the position.

Captain Cochran said, "Allow them in."

Ephraim returned, accompanied by four men. He then exited immediately. They introduced themselves as Samuel Clark, John Simpson, Robert White and Matthew Bell.

"Gentlemen, I assume you have come about the job?" Captain Cochran said, standing before the men.

Matthew Bell spoke up, "Job? No, we had some time and thought we'd pay a social call. We heard that Stephen and Henry were visiting."

Jack was suddenly suspicious of the men in the room. He looked at his mother. Her eyes were locked on the men from New Castle.

The captain visibly stiffened. "A social call? I've been at this post for nearly four years and have never had social callers." He turned to Batson, his voice, accusing. "You told me you came about the position as lightkeeper."

Jack's mother crossed into the room. She leaned close and whispered to Jack, "Stay here with your father."

She quickly slipped out of the gathering room.

Isaac appeared at the door. He was agitated. He spoke rapidly and his voice was loud, "Sir, we've spotted four to five men approaching the fort from different sides. We don't know who they are."

Cochran ordered, "Do not allow them into the fort."

"Yes Sir!"

Captain Cochran turned to the men in his home. His eyes were narrowed to mere slits, his hands gripped into fists. "State your business with me."

The men looked at one another. Batson opened his mouth to speak. But before he could answer, Sarah Cochran burst through the doorway. Flames from the fire glinted off a pistol she held tightly in one hand. She handed the weapon to her husband then immediately left the room through the front door leaving it open.

Captain Cochran pointed the pistol at the men.

The New Castle men, visibly startled by the appearance of a weapon, backed away from the captain — one knocking into a wooden chair.

Simpson said, "We don't want any trouble Captain."

Cochran angrily shouted, "I repeat! State your business!"

Ephraim now stood in the open front doorway. His musket was leveled at the men. "Mrs. Cochran said you needed me."

"Yes Guard! Remove these men, but separate them! I don't want them sharing stories."

"Yes, Sir!" Ephraim continued to aim his weapon.

Captain Cochran said, "I wish to speak with John Simpson first."

"Move!" Ephraim commanded. The others hurried outside as Ephraim pointed his musket at them.

Isaac now appeared in the doorway, out of breath and pale, he managed to say, "Sir, men are coming in all directions!"

The captain shouted, "Don't allow anyone else inside the fort!"

His face showed no emotion as he eyed John Simpson. "Sit!" He kicked a wooden chair towards Simpson who immediately sat down. The captain remained on his feet, gripping the pistol, but not threatening with it. Standing over Simpson he demanded, "Tell me why you are here!"

Simpson looked up at Captain Cochran, his eyes wide. Jack saw beads of sweat on his forehead. "Captain, I have no idea why the other men came. I simply wished to make a social call."

"Why?" Captain Cochran's voice was tinged with distrust. "Why after four years at this post, did you decide to pay a social visit?"

John Simpson said, "I heard you will be leaving the fort, soon."

"Leave the fort?" Captain Cochran straightened as confusion crossed his face. "Where did you hear that? I know of no such thing. I plan to remain in command at His Majesty's Castle William and Mary."

Simpson said, "It's what I heard."

Captain Cochran's eyes flashed with rage. "You're lying! Get up!" Then he shouted, "Guard! Bring me Robert White!"

Robert White was brought in as John Simpson was escorted out. They had only a moment to catch each other's eye. Simpson shook his head slightly and Jack took it as a signal to White.

Captain Cochran strode over to White, circling him, all the while looking him up and down. He said, "Simpson told me your plan."

Robert White's eyes widened but he didn't speak.

Jack's eyes widened, too. Simpson hadn't told his father anything about a plan.

Captain Cochran moved in close, still holding the pistol to his side. "You and the other men plan to take the fort! Admit it!"

White stared back at the captain.

"Admit it!" Cochran raged.

White answered, "Yes, yes, it's true. The men are here to take control of the fort."

"Traitors!" Captain Cochran spat the word at Robert White. "The whole lot of you! You're nothing but traitors!" Anger raising to a boiling point, the captain raised his pistol and pointed it directly at White. "I have no intention of being taken prisoner in my own fort! Get out! Now!"

White hurried out, not looking back.

Captain Cochran called out, "Guard!"

Ephraim appeared in the doorway.

"Escort the men out of the fort immediately!"

"Yes Sir!"

"Why did you let them go?" Jack's anger wasn't masked. "They were trying to trick us! They wanted to take control of the fort!"

"Son, we have to try to reason with them." Captain Cochran's eyes met Jack's. "Taking the men prisoner would only inflame the situation. I can only hope they will rethink their plan and go home now that they know I will not hand over control of the fort. But we must prepare in case they don't. Let's go!"

HIS MAJESTY'S CASTLE WILLIAM AND MARY
2:45 P.M.

♕ ♕ ♕

Men burst through the gate of His Majesty's Castle William and Mary. Andrew couldn't tell if they were pushed out or chased out by the guards. The soldiers now raised their muskets, pointing them at the men outside the fort. Andrew swallowed hard as he realized, the soldiers' muskets were pointed at him!

Joseph stood next to him near the front gate. As far as Andrew could see were New Hampshire and Massachusetts men ready to remove gunpowder. Many were still arriving. Crossing to the fort, Andrew had remained hopeful that they could remove the powder peacefully, as they had in Rhode Island. But now. . .

Captain Cochran's orders to his men rang out over the walls of the fort. His words pulled the air from Andrew's lungs.

"To your stations!" he called. "Make ready two field cannons and point them up the river! We must stop the men who are still landing!"

Andrew's head reeled as he looked toward the river. Men were still coming on gundalows, scows and barges.

Captain Cochran shouted again, "Position one cannon toward the gate!"

Gasps from the men standing with Andrew cut through the frigid air as they realized a cannon was being directed at them at point blank range! Andrew felt boxed in as men began to push in different directions to get away from the gate and the path of a cannonball.

"Back away from the gate!" A guard yelled out. His voice was loud, but trembled slightly.

"Back away!" the guard yelled again, his voice stronger now. He pointed his musket at them.

Through the slats, Andrew watched two soldiers wheel a cannon to the front gate.

Jeers erupted from some in the mob and men pushed toward the gate, defying the order, and pushing Andrew along with them.

"Surrender or die!" someone called out to the soldiers.

More jeers followed from the angry men outside the fort. Joseph joined with them.

"Back away!" This time the command came from outside the gate. It was John Langdon. Wrapped in a black cloak, he stepped into an opening in the mass of men. "Move away from the gate! We don't want a bloody confrontation like the one in Boston!"

The forward movement halted.

In Boston, several years back, they called it a massacre of innocent civilians. Andrew had seen an engraving of it by Paul Revere. It was a horrible scene — British soldiers firing at innocent people at pointblank range. But some said the soldier who fired was provoked by the crowd.

Andrew pushed the thought out of his mind. He didn't want to think that could happen here.

The men grew quiet and moved back from the gate, but the soldier kept his weapon pointed at them.

Andrew recognized Captain Wolcott standing to one side. He and about twelve men approached the sentry at the gate again.

"Stop where you are!" The sentry demanded, his musket pointed through the slatted gate ready to fire.

The men stopped as ordered and Captain Wolcott spoke, "We wish to talk with Captain Cochran."

"Do not come any closer."

Captain Cochran, now at the gate demanded, "What do you want?"

John Langdon spoke up, "Captain Cochran, I wish to speak directly with you. Please allow me and one other man inside."

Joseph angrily kicked his toe at the frozen ground.

The seconds it took Captain Cochran to decide seemed endless. Andrew shivered from the cold and from fear.

Finally the sentry lowered his weapon and opened the gate. Captain Cochran directed, "Two men only."

John Langdon and Robert White had barely stepped into the fort when shouts came from the angry men outside the gate. "Surrender or die! Surrender or die!"

Joseph lunged forward and repeated the chant. "Surrender or die!"

The terror on the soldiers' faces as they slammed the gate to His Majesty's Castle William and Mary stabbed Andrew as sharply as the blade of a bayonet. He understood their fear. He felt it too.

Inside the fort, the two men stood before Captain Cochran. Jack remained at his father's side. This time there were no handshakes. Jack recognized the tall man wrapped in the cloak as John Langdon from Portsmouth.

The captain stood rigidly, his demeanor abrupt. "State your business, Langdon."

John Langdon spoke, "Captain Cochran. I will not pretend to have any business with you except for the truth. We are here to take possession of all the gunpowder in the fort's magazine."

Captain Cochran, keeping his anger in check, replied, "If you have the appropriate paperwork from Governor Wentworth, I will release the gunpowder to you immediately."

Langdon was equally abrupt. "I do not have any paperwork, but make no mistake, we will leave with the gunpowder."

"I cannot give you the powder!" Bubbling anger rose in Captain Cochran's voice. "Your request is absurd!"

"The powder belongs to us!" John Langdon was clear. He looked the captain straight in the eye as he told him, "This is not a request. The gunpowder belongs to the people of New Hampshire. We will take it at any cost!"

Captain Cochran did not back down. "If that is the case, then you will have to take the gunpowder by force. Now get out!"

"As you wish Captain," Langdon told him calmly. "We will leave." His gaze locked on the captain, he added, "But mark my words, we will take the gunpowder with us."

Captain Cochran leaned forward, his words deliberate. "If any of those men outside attempt to come into the fort, their blood will be on your hands for I will fire upon them!"

"Guard!" he called. "Remove these men!"

Captain Cochran turned to Jack and ordered, "Get our muskets!"

Jack rushed to retrieve muskets, bayonets and cartridge boxes then ran back to his father.

Captain Cochran, with a pistol in his hand, shouted orders to his soldiers, "Man your stations!" To Jack he said, "Join the soldiers."

"Yes, Captain!"

Captain Cochran wasted no time ordering his men, "Ready the muskets!"

The soldiers loaded their muskets with speed and precision. They were a small contingent of full-time militiamen but a well-trained one, always prepared to defend the fort.

Jack opened his cartridge box. The paper cartridges were packed with black powder and a musket ball for quick loading. He bit off the end of a cartridge and poured a small amount of powder into the pan. Next, he dropped the cartridge, powder end first, into the barrel, and using a rammer, he shoved the cartridge down the barrel. Jack then secured his bayonet to the end of his Brown Bess musket.

Captain Cochran shouted more orders, stationing his soldiers at various points. Well aware of the fort's weaknesses, he positioned the few men in the areas of greatest concern.

Jack took his place on a platform along the wall. Disturbed by what was to come, he gripped his loaded musket, ready to use it upon command.

In the silent frigid air, Captain Cochran issued one more order,

"Do not flinch on pain of death! Defend the fort at all costs!"

A chill traveled through Jack's spine.

Shouts of fear came from the men outside the gate as they looked down the barrel of the four-pounder. Jack watched men scatter, pushing to get out of the way of the cannon. Ephraim stood by the cannon, ready to fire directly at those who tried to enter through the front gate.

Jack struggled to stay in control of his rising anger and fear. In all his years at the fort, no soldier had ever fired a weapon at an enemy. But now they pointed cannon and muskets at their neighbors.

Jack swung his musket into a ready position. He was prepared to defend the fort.

Within an instant an order rang out from outside the gate, "STORM THE FORT!"

HIS MAJESTY'S CASTLE WILLIAM AND MARY
3:00 P.M.

꒰ꔛ꒱ ꒰ꔛ꒱ ꒰ꔛ꒱

Captain Cochran commanded, "FIRE!"

Cannons exploded instantly, blinding Jack.

Four-pound balls hurled out of each cannon, one out the gate and two at the raiders still on the river. The deafening booms surrounded him. Jack struggled to focus his eyes. He blinked several times, clearing his vision. He turned and watched as the cannon ball shot out the gate bounced on the ground. Men ran in all directions desperately trying to escape its deadly path.

He turned back and pointed his musket toward the men charging toward the wall. Jack fired into the mob of men from New Hampshire and Massachusetts. The musket kicked back hard, wrenching his shoulder. In the smoke and chaos, he didn't know if he had hit any of the raiders.

Despite the cannon and musket fire, men knocked down part of the earthen wall as they rushed the fort. Climbing quickly, they were trying to slip under the guns before the soldiers could reload.

Jack tried to reload his musket. His fingers were cold and his hands trembled. But anger now boiled through him. Steadying his hands through sheer determination, he loaded as he vowed to himself that he would protect the powder and weapons for King George.

Men were pouring over the walls.

Jack heard shouts around him, but they were muffled. Ephraim yelled something to him but Jack could not make out the words. Then Ephraim pointed, signaling that Jack should help defend the gate. Jack ran from his location and repositioned himself on the platform by the gate where more men were entering the fort. Looking down, he saw Isaac wrestle with a raider who had grabbed his musket. The men struggled, but Isaac would not give up his weapon. The man pushed Isaac, but Isaac held tight to his musket, wrenching it away from the man. Suddenly Captain Thomas Palmer, a raider, jumped between the two. He pointed his gun at Isaac!

Palmer fired!

Jack cried out as he saw a flash from the pistol. Palmer had fired at Isaac at point blank range.

Jack turned away. He couldn't bear to watch Isaac Seveay crumple to the ground. But he didn't hear the crack of a pistol firing.

Jack looked down.

The pistol hadn't discharged. Jack wondered if the weapon was loaded. Captain Palmer's pistol was now pointed in Isaac's face. He shouted at Isaac, "Fall to your knees! Beg for pardon for resisting us!"

Isaac Seveay's eyes blazed in rage and defiance. "I will kneel when my legs are cut off below the knees, but not before!"

Palmer delivered a blow with his pistol that knocked Isaac to the ground, and several men attacked Isaac, one man punching him in the head with his fists.

Jack jumped down from his place on the firing platform to help Isaac as he was being pummeled.

Andrew shoved his way through the mob, not sure where he was. There was chaos in all directions. He had been pushed through the gate as men surged into the fort after the cannon was fired. Now men swarmed everywhere.

Shouting from the middle of the compound stopped him in his tracks. Andrew turned to see a soldier fighting with three, no, four men. One of the men shouted, "Surrender Hall!"

Ephraim Hall hung tightly to his musket using the handle to punch at his attackers. He hit one man in the face. Blood spewed profusely from a gapping wound on the man's forehead.

Another from the mob screamed at the soldier, "If I had a club, I'd knock—"

More shouts drowned out the threat.

Then a man grabbed the barrel of the musket in the soldier's hand.

Andrew held his breath, waiting to hear the firearm discharge as they wrestled and fell to the ground. Three other men now pounced and ripped the weapon from Hall's hands.

Men grabbed the soldier's arms as he continued to resist. With difficulty, they were able to subdue Ephraim Hall. In a fury, the man whose face was covered with blood, smashed Hall's musket on the ground.

Turmoil mounting in another part of the fort caught Andrew's eye. He now saw Jack's father, Captain Cochran, up against a wall, surrounded by menacing men.

The captain, his bayonet attached to his musket, struggled against overwhelming odds. He lunged, jabbing one man in the arm. The man screamed in pain as he fell backwards.

Surrounding men cried out, "Get the bayonet! Get the bayonet!"

Suddenly, Thomas Pickering, a sailor Andrew recognized as a man from Portsmouth, scaled the wall as the other rebels fought to overpower Captain Cochran.

When he reached the top, Pickering jumped on to the captain's shoulders swinging one arm around his neck. Captain Cochran stumbled but did not fall. He struggled to get the man off his back by pounding him against the wall, but Pickering held on tight.

Cochran slammed Pickering into the wall one more time. The captain twisted, causing the man to fall to the ground, but the captain fell to the ground with Pickering. Cochran grabbed his wrist, wincing in pain.

Suddenly, Jack came from nowhere on a dead run.

He hit one of the men in the midsection with the butt of his musket. The man dropped to the ground. Jack swung again, catching another in the shoulder before five large men overpowered him, angrily stripping the musket out of his hands.

A mob surrounded the fallen captain. Jeering and taunting, they closed in on the captain as a voice gave an order, "Give us the keys to the powder house!"

"No!" Captain Cochran replied.

John Langdon demanded, "Get him up!"

Two men grabbed Captain Cochran, pulled him to his feet and held his arms. Cochran tried to wrest away from the men, but they held him tight.

Langdon stood close to the captain and demanded again, "Give us the keys to the powder house!"

Captain Cochran, his eyes mere slits, bellowed in Langdon's face, "You might as well ask for my life instead of the keys. I would just as soon part with that!"

John Langdon stared back into the eyes of the captain of the fort, then stepped away and issued an order, "Take Captain Cochran and his son to the barracks!"

The men began pushing the captain and Jack. The captain dug in his heels. The men holding him stumbled, almost losing their grip. Jack slumped suddenly and pulled away, but was grabbed immediately.

A cry rang out, "Look out behind!"

Andrew turned to see Sarah Cochran, Jack's mother. She had picked up her husband's fallen musket with a bayonet attached and charged the men who held her husband and son.

In the frenzy, they let go of the captives. Captain Cochran threw several punches with his good hand as Jack, wedged in tight, rammed an elbow into a man's gut, forcing him to double over. But another man immediately wrapped his arms around Jack.

Mrs. Cochran jabbed the bayonet at the men, barely missing one who dove away from her. She lunged again, but three men came up from behind. Two grabbed her arms and the third yanked the musket away.

A raider twisted the captain's injured wrist behind his back. Pain transformed Captain Cochran's face.

"Take them to the barracks!" The angry voice belonged to John Langdon. "And take the other soldiers to the barracks as well!"

Mrs. Cochran, struggling against her captors, demanded, "Let me or our son go back to the house. Our young children are in there and are probably frightened."

Langdon hesitated for a moment, considering the request.

Someone said, "It's a trick! You can't trust them! One of us should watch their children!"

"No!" Jack shouted struggling against the man who pinned his arms.

Andrew stepped forward and said, "Sir, please let me. I'll watch the children."

Andrew hoped Jack would take some comfort in the fact that he would be there for the younger brother and sisters.

Andrew repeated the request, "Mr. Langdon, please allow me to watch the children. I know Jack. He is my friend."

Langdon looked uncertain and Andrew realized he should not have told Langdon that he and Jack were friends. Perhaps Mr. Langdon would not trust him to watch them.

Jack stopped struggling and stared at Andrew, his face suddenly contorted in rage. "Andrew Beckett. You are not my friend! You are a traitor! I hope you swing from the gallows!"

Andrew stood wide-eyed, shocked by Jack's response.

John Langdon, no longer uncertain, nodded to Andrew. "You can watch the children. They will be less frightened by you than one of the men."

Andrew was frozen in place.

Jack launched another verbal attack, "Traitors! All of you!"

Langdon commanded, "Take them to the barracks!"

The men pulled their captives toward the barracks. Jack's voice still shouted insults and threats.

"Extinguish the fires in the barracks and house!" Langdon commanded. "Get our powder!"

Men cheered and ran to the powder house.

"Go!" Langdon barked at Andrew.

HIS MAJESTY'S CASTLE WILLIAM AND MARY

3:15 P.M.

👑 👑 👑

Andrew turned and ran from the sight of Jack and his parents being forced to the barracks. And he ran from Jack's words. Jack had said they were not friends. Jack had called him a traitor. But they had to remove the powder so that all of the citizens would be safe once the British regulars arrived at the fort.

As Andrew ran toward the house, he heard Langdon's voice behind him. "Pry the door open with a crowbar! Then start removing the powder. We need to act quickly. The King's troops could arrive anytime!"

Andrew felt he was swimming upstream as he pushed through the fort swarming with men. "To the powder house!" came the shouts as the men moved in the opposite direction.

Andrew was almost at the Cochran's house when he heard a commotion. The cheers of men roared nearby, "HUZZA! HUZZA! HUZZA!"

He thought the cheers would have come from opening the powder house, but they rose from another part of the fort. Andrew turned toward the chant, searching through the smoke that still filled the air. He wanted to know what ignited the celebration.

A light snow was falling and the haze cleared just enough to see. But the sight sent a chill to Andrew's core. The enormous flag, measuring the height of five men by three men, was more than halfway down the ship's mast that served as a flagpole! The King's flag that had flown for over one hundred years declaring British control over Portsmouth Harbor was being hauled down by John Palmer, the son of Captain Thomas Palmer.

Andrew could not breathe as he realized what the men had done. This was no longer a run to seize gunpowder for the protection of the people of the province. This was an attack on a royal fort and therefore an attack on the British Crown! Jack Cochran was right. This was treason! They could all swing from the gallows!

Andrew saw Joseph run toward the flag as it was coming down. He leapt up, his full weight hung on the King's colors as he and others pulled down the massive flag.

Andrew suddenly felt sick. He half-stumbled the rest of the way to the Cochran's dwelling. He opened the door to Jack's home and closed it quickly, shutting out the horror outside. He was sweating, even shaking. He tried to calm down.

He struggled to stay composed. Right now, he had to take care of Jack's younger siblings. Maybe one day, Andrew hoped, when Jack had a chance to think through what had happened, he would understand and appreciate that Andrew took care of his little brother and sisters. But at that moment, Andrew wished he had paid more attention when Jack talked about his family. How old were the children? He knew they were younger than thirteen-year old Jack. *They must be frightened*, he thought.

The children were not in immediate view. Flames blazed in the fireplace in the center of the room as if it had been attended throughout the struggle. He smelled stew cooking. It was likely the family's dinner — never eaten.

It was at that moment that Andrew heard a click to his left side.

He turned slowly, already quite certain what had produced the unmistakable sound. Standing was a girl, maybe nine or ten. She held a pistol with both hands. It was pointed right at him.

Andrew did not take another step.

Behind her he now saw a small boy with silky blond hair.

The boy smiled sweetly at Andrew as he said, "You better not move. Sally shoots better than my brother Jack."

Andrew looked beyond them. Another little girl stared at him.

"My name is Andrew. I attend the Latin Grammar School with your brother, Jack. He's my friend," Andrew told them, careful not to say that he was Jack's friend since Jack had just told him that he was not. "I came to see if you are alright."

The girl named Sally held the gun steady. Andrew wasn't certain if she had blinked. He spoke directly to her. "I have some maple candy in my pocket," he said. "I'll give you and your brother and sister each a piece."

Sally still hadn't blinked.

Andrew added, "If you don't shoot me."

HIS MAJESTY'S CASTLE WILLIAM AND MARY
4:30 P.M.

♛ ♛ ♛

Andrew waded through the icy water to the loaded gundalow. His feet and ankles throbbed with each step.

"Move!" a man shouted at him. "The tide is shifting!"

Andrew knew they needed to catch the changing tide to travel inland but he was going as fast as he could. He bit his lip, stopping himself from engaging in an unpleasant exchange. He was half-frozen, exhausted both physically and mentally. He had no desire to be in the frigid water any longer than necessary.

Hands grabbed each of his and pulled him up, dripping into the waiting gundalow. Weighted down by barrels of gunpowder, surprisingly the flat bottom of the barge didn't sink below the waterline. But gundalows were made to carry very heavy loads.

"Let's go or we'll be here all night!" a man Andrew didn't know urged.

The sky was darkening and the temperature was dropping quickly. Andrew believed it to be close to 4:30. The sun had set, but there was still light in the sky. The entire raid, from landing at the fort to securing the powder, may have lasted less than two hours, he judged. But to Andrew it had seemed like days.

"Drew!" the shout came from on shore. Andrew recognized the voice. It was Joseph calling out to him.

Andrew cringed. He couldn't get the image of Joseph pulling down the King's colors out of his head.

"Drew!" The shout was even louder.

Andrew reached over a barrel for a sweep. Thankfully, the gundalow left the shoreline. Where it was bound, he didn't know. And at that moment, he didn't care. The day's events were a jumble of confusion in his aching head.

The gundalow, carrying barrels of powder from the fort, slowly made its way along the river. Few men spoke, but Andrew was able to find out that his group was headed back to Portsmouth, and then would travel by cart inland to the town of Durham. Other barrels of gunpowder were bound for other towns. He heard some of the barrels were on the way to Exeter, some to Dover. That way, if some shipments were blocked or confiscated, some of the powder would remain in the hands of the citizens of the province.

Some talked, but most were quiet, probably as tired as Andrew. The men on board were tense, not as jubilant as he had expected. Andrew was glad because he did not take any joy in the raid.

Freezing and weary, he now sat with his back braced against a barrel. The sweep lay next to him, ready if needed. Andrew's breeches and stockings were caked with ice from the knees down. He brushed them off. His mind and body ached as the gundalow drifted in the dark and his thoughts drifted to the raid.

While he'd watched the Cochran children, men had loaded barrels of gunpowder on to gundalows, scows and any other barge that could carry the load. He knew the men had taken one hundred barrels, and as they left the fort, they had freed the prisoners.

Andrew couldn't get the Cochran children out of his mind, especially Sally. She wasn't at all frightened while he was with them. She had finally lowered the pistol and let him give candy to the younger two, but the pistol remained in her hands, and she did not accept a piece of candy.

He leaned his head back, closed his eyes, and tried to clear his thoughts.

Andrew's head banged against a barrel of gunpowder, jolting him and he realized he had somehow fallen asleep as they traveled inland by cart.

"Where are we?" he asked too loudly. He was surprised he'd slept in the freezing outdoors. But never in his life had he felt so tired. He massaged his stiff neck, then his shoulder.

Earlier in the evening, they had arrived in Portsmouth. As the gundalow reached the dock, two men jumped from the barge to the small pier. With ropes they pulled the gundalow closer to the dock. Ice cracked and shattered as the heavy load broke through the shallow frozen water.

Waiting on shore were horse and ox drawn carts and carriages, enough to carry the gunpowder barrels from Andrew's gundalow and those to follow to their final inland destinations. With so many men, it didn't take long to move the heavy barrels on to the carts and begin the slow ride inland.

A voice said, "We're in Durham at Major John Sullivan's house."

Durham was a small town several miles upriver where the Piscataqua met the Oyster River. Andrew's eyes were drawn to the yellow light coming from the small windows of a building near the water's edge. The clouds had parted briefly and in the fleeting moonlight he made out the outline of a colonial home, rectangular with a flat front. The smell of burning wood cut through the cold air.

The front door of the house opened, more light poured out and Andrew was able to make out the figure of a man. He moved quickly toward the cart. A young man, Andrew decided.

The voice in the distance demanded, "Who is there! Answer immediately!" In the moonlight Andrew saw that the man pointed a musket at them!

A man on board the cart shouted back, "We are here to see Major Sullivan! We are here on orders of Captain John Langdon! It is urgent that we speak with him. May I approach?"

"No!" His answer came quickly. "Wait here."

The man on cart did not accept the abrupt response. He shouted back, "Who are you? How dare you interfere! It is urgent that I speak with Major Sullivan!"

The voice in the darkness said, "My name is Scammell — Alexander Scammell. I read law with Major Sullivan. I will let him know you are here." Musket aimed, he ordered, "I repeat! Wait here!" The man named Scammell ran the short distance back to the house.

Andrew knew of John Sullivan. He was a major in the provincial militia and a Durham attorney. He had represented New Hampshire as a delegate to the Continental Congress in Philadelphia. Andrew was there, in October, when Sullivan spoke to the people of Portsmouth upon his return to New Hampshire. He recalled a man with a dark complexion, black hair and black eyes who stood tall. He spoke with great passion and confidence to the assembled crowd about the decisions made by the Continental Congress.

Andrew's eyes now scanned the landscape. The house, set back from the water had a structure behind. The billowing smoke from the chimney of the house looked inviting. Andrew wished he was nearing his own house and a warm fire.

A man next to him said, "Get up. I see Sullivan walking toward us."

Andrew jumped up and a groan escaped his lips. The soreness of his muscles caused by moving barrels of gunpowder from the gundalow to the cart, tore through his legs. He rubbed his left calf and looked out at the man who made his way toward them. Even in the dimming moonlight, he saw a man who moved with determination. Reaching them, Sullivan stopped and examined the cart.

"A call for support has gone out to Nathaniel Folsom in Exeter," a man informed Major Sullivan.

Andrew knew the name. Nathaniel Folsom was the other New Hampshire delegate to the Continental Congress who had traveled to Philadelphia with Major Sullivan.

"For what purpose have you called for assistance?" Major Sullivan eyed the barrels on board the cart. Andrew saw the major's eyes widen. "Are those barrels of gunpowder?"

"Yes Sir!" the man answered. "We received word that two regiments of the King's soldiers have been dispatched to Castle William and Mary to take over the fort."

Major Sullivan's words were as cold as the air. "What have you done?"

Andrew waited for the answer.

HOME OF ROYAL GOVERNOR JOHN WENTWORTH
8:20 P.M.

♕ ♕ ♕

Jack and Ephraim struggled to control the barge as they guided it into South Mill Pond in Portsmouth from the strong current of the Piscataqua River. The barge still maintained momentum from the tide and it rocked precariously. With only dim moonlight to illuminate their surroundings, they used poles to keep the barge from ramming the shore.

The water lapped against the shoreline as they created a surge in the shallow water. Working in tandem, they didn't dare speak. Traitors, the name Jack had given the men who raided the fort, could be anywhere along the shore, waiting, watching, especially as they neared Governor Wentworth's home.

In spite of the injured shoulder, Ephraim suffered during the attack on the fort, he volunteered to go with Jack to deliver a message to Governor Wentworth. Jack's anger still raged. In addition to Ephraim's injury, the other soldiers were bruised and bloodied. His father's wrist was severely sprained, perhaps broken. Worse, the traitors had stolen the powder the soldiers needed to protect the people. They threatened to return and take the rest of the King's property. They even declared they would raid the Treasury!

Jack, his parents and the soldiers were released from the barracks after the men left the fort. When Jack returned to the house, the children were sitting around the table, unharmed. He was grateful for that. But what happened next played over in his mind during the long, cold crossing to South Mill Pond.

Upon entering the house, Jack saw William holding a piece of candy. "Where did you get that?" Jack demanded. He knew William would have eaten all the candy he had given him.

William froze, his eyes wide. Jack rarely raised his voice to his younger brother. "That boy, Andrew, gave it to us," he stammered.

Jack grabbed the remaining sticky candy from William's hand and threw it into the fire shouting, "We don't take anything from traitors!"

"I thought he was your friend." William stifled a sob.

"He's not my friend. He is a traitor! He'll hang one day!"

William's eyes brimmed with tears, but he didn't cry.

Jack's visit had been brief, and he now regretted leaving without saying goodbye to his younger brother.

The barge glided to Governor Wentworth's wooden dock on South Mill Pond. Ephraim winced in pain as he suddenly moved the pole to prevent the barge from crashing into the dock.

Jack jumped off and secured the barge loosely for a quick getaway.

"I'll come back and let you know if I'm returning to the fort with you," Jack whispered.

"Be careful." Ephraim whispered back. "I'm sure the house is being watched. I don't know what they might do to you if—"

Jack cut him off, not wanting to think of the possibility. "I'll be careful."

Jack ran through the dormant garden at the back of the property to the large white house the governor called the Hut. At the corner of the house, he looked up and down the street. Convinced he was alone, Jack approached the large front door and knocked as loud as he dared.

One of the governor's English servants called through the thick wooden door, "State your business."

"Jack Cochran. I'm the son of Captain John Cochran from His Majesty's Castle William and Mary with an urgent message for Governor Wentworth."

The door opened slightly at first. Yellow candlelight lit Jack's face. Then it swung open wide allowing Jack to enter. Shutting and locking the door in one motion, the Englishman said, "Come with me."

They moved quickly through the house to the governor's office. Governor Wentworth sat at a large wooden desk, head bent, engrossed in work. He seemed not to notice that they had entered the room.

Mrs. Wentworth sat nearby. She looked up at Jack, but did not speak.

"Jack Cochran to see you, Sir."

The governor looked up, seemingly startled. He appeared tired and stood up slowly.

"Come in Jack," the governor's voice was tense.

The servant disappeared.

Jack bowed to Mrs. Wentworth. In the yellow candlelight of the room, he saw that her hands were gripped together. Jack was certain the governor and his wife had already heard about the raid on His Majesty's Castle.

Jack took a few steps toward the Governor and handed him the letter that he carried in his pocket. "Your Excellency. I have an urgent message from my father."

The governor took the letter and moved nearer the candle on his desk. He read it silently.

May it please your Excellency:

I received your Excellency's favour of yesterday, and in obedience thereto kept a strict watch all night. . . . Nothing material occurred till this day, . . . I prepared to make the best defense I could, and pointed some guns to those places where I expected they would enter. About three o'clock, the fort was beset on all sides by upwards of four hundred men. I told them on their peril not to enter. They replied they would. I immediately ordered three four pounders to be fired on them, and then the small arms; and, before we could be ready to fire again, we were stormed on all quarters, and they immediately secured both me and my men, and kept us prisoners for about one hour and a half, during which time they broke open the powder-house, and took all the powder away, except

119

one barrel; and having put it into boats and sent it off, they released me from confinement. To which I can only add, that I did all in my power to defend this fort, but all my efforts could not avail against so great a number.

I am your Excellency's, etc.,
(Signed)   John Cochran

Reaching a hand up, the governor rubbed his forehead just above his eyes. His voice was tight, as if he was trying to control his anger. "I had received word of some trouble, but I never believed it would come to this."

He turned to Jack, sudden alarm in his face. "Was anyone injured, or—?"

He stopped abruptly and moved quickly to Mrs. Wentworth. He reached for her hand. "My dear, I think you should rest. Why don't you go upstairs and lie down."

Mrs. Wentworth simply nodded, not speaking a word. He helped her up from the chair and they walked together, arm in arm, out of the office. Jack heard the governor call for a servant to help Mrs. Wentworth upstairs.

He returned quickly. As he closed the door to the room he said, "Jack, sit down. Please tell me everything that happened."

Jack sat on a chair near the governor's desk. The governor sat down, and leaned toward Jack. Concern filled his light eyes.

"Jack, is your family safe?"

Jack's mouth was suddenly dry. So much had happened. He was

angry, but he hadn't had time to think about what might have been. "Yes, Your Excellency, my mother, brother and sisters are well. My father's wrist was sprained, or perhaps broken, but that was the most serious injury. The soldiers are bruised."

"Were any of the raiders—?" he didn't finish the sentence.

"I don't know Sir. I believe some were injured, but they all disappeared."

The governor sat back, appearing somewhat relieved. He stared at the pine floorboards at his feet.

His eyes returned to Jack's as anger bubbled up. "This powder run should never have happened."

"Your Excellency, I don't understand why they took the powder."

"Paul Revere!" His anger was now fully on the surface. "Revere brought word that British regulars were on the way to take over the Castle!"

"What?" Jack was taken aback.

"It's not true, Jack. Let me assure you. Your father would have been told if regulars were on the way. But the townspeople believed it." The governor gripped his hands into fists, releasing them then gripping again. "I wanted to go to the tavern yesterday and try to talk with the leaders when I first heard about Revere's message, but was advised against it. My council members said many of the men were drinking and it would be dangerous."

He sat back, regret etched in his face. "I should not have listened to them. I thought only a few drunk men might go to the fort last night. That's why I alerted your father, but I never thought a mob would actually take part in a powder run."

Shaking his head in frustration, Governor Wentworth said, "When nothing occurred last night, we thought cooler heads had prevailed, but at noon when we heard the drums in the street—" His voice trailed off. "I tried to take a barge to the fort, but my own bargemen wouldn't take me! They were too frightened."

Jack said, "Sir, it was more than a powder run."

The governor looked up at Jack. The flames from the nearby candle flickered in his narrowing eyes. "What do you mean?"

"Your Excellency, the men that raided the fort hauled down the King's colors."

The governor's body rocked backwards, shifting his chair. "The flag?" he shouted, suddenly on his feet. "They hauled down the King's flag?"

"Yes Your Excellency. They hauled down King George's flag."

The governor raged. "That is outrageous! That is treason!"

Jack fueled the governor's anger. "I heard some say they will come back to the fort and take the rest of the arms and cannon. They said they would even raid the Treasury!"

"Raid the Treasury?" Governor Wentworth paced the room furiously. "Treason!"

He spun around and faced Jack. "Trying to secure powder they believed belonged to the province was wrong, but perhaps understandable given the false information provided by that silversmith, Revere. But to haul down the King's flag? To threaten the Treasury? There's no explanation save one! Treason!"

Suddenly, he stopped and asked, "What has your father told you to do after delivering this message?"

"Sir, if you have a response I will take it to him. Ephraim Hall is waiting at the dock. If not, Ephraim will return to the fort and I will stay at my grandparents' home in town."

Governor Wentworth nodded as he told Jack, "I have an important express to write, but not one for your father. Go to your grandparents' house. I will send a servant with you. It is not safe for you to walk the streets alone."

He stood directly in front of Jack and placed both hands on the boy's shoulders. "I will take action! Come to my office at the State House tomorrow and I will have instructions for you to take to your father."

THE STATE HOUSE
December 15, 1774
2:00 P.M.

Sheriff Parker lunged through the council chamber door announcing, "There are hundreds of men on the streets! It appears that Major John Sullivan and men from Durham have joined them." He barely took a breath before adding, "And worse, I heard that five hundred more men are on the way. They are intent on raiding the fort, again! This time they plan to seize the cannons!"

The men in the room, including the governor's council and other magistrates, exchanged worried looks.

Jack stood near an upstairs window of the State House, and looked down on to the Parade below. A slight gasp escaped his lips, but no one in the chamber heard. He had never seen so many men gathered together.

He had left his grandparents' shortly after 10:00 in the morning. He had kept his head down, collar up and hat pulled low. A cold rain was falling so no one took notice.

Governor Wentworth paced, the pine floorboards creaking with every step. He spoke rapidly. "We must take action now." He spun around facing the men in the chamber. "The sheer number of men who have converged upon Portsmouth make it impossible to protect the Castle or the Treasury without further troop support."

He made the statement that Jack and everyone in the room knew. Not only could they not reasonably believe they could protect the fort from a further raid, they could not likely protect themselves. Angry men were swarming the normally quiet streets of Portsmouth.

The governor said, "We must immediately enlist thirty men to try to protect His Majesty's Castle. Assemble them. I will lead them to the fort myself! Call for my barge!"

The men looked uncomfortably at one another before Chief Justice Theodore Atkinson spoke, "Governor, it is unlikely that we can find thirty men who will willingly go against the masses of men on the street."

The royal governor, anger boiling, raged, "Revere and the rebels in Boston are responsible for this madness! General Gage did not send soldiers to take over the Castle! This was an intentional lie designed to stir the good people of the province into a frenzy!" With eyes narrowed he accused, "I should have gone to the tavern!"

"Governor Wentworth," Mr. Penhallow spoke sharply. "What could you have said to calm their fears?"

"I could have told them that Gage had not sent troops!"

Sheriff Parker turned from the window and said, "Sir, you know it would not have been prudent to have gone to the tavern. Tempers were high. They had just learned the information. That combined with rum and ale, it would have been a mistake."

The Governor resumed pacing. His footsteps pounded the floorboards. "Sheriff Parker," the governor stopped pacing. "Your services would be of better use out amongst the people."

"Sir, I disagree." The sheriff responded with his eyes again on the street below. "It is my duty to protect you."

"No one has threatened me!"

"Not yet, Sir."

Jack watched as both John Fenton and Samuel Penhallow exchanged worried glances. It was true. No one had threatened Governor Wentworth's physical wellbeing, but the citizens had never been so stirred up. Jack understood the sheriff's concern.

Governor Wentworth commenced pacing. "Sheriff Parker! You are hereby ordered to inform the officers of the militia to call out their men!"

"Sir—"

"Do not question me! Do it! It is an order!"

The Sheriff snapped to attention. "Yes Sir!"

"And find Major Sullivan! Bring him to me!"

Andrew pulled his collar up and moved through the crowds of men in the street. He heard bits and pieces of conversations as he passed. They were preparing to take action again. Andrew kept moving, walking through the growing group of men. He searched the faces and recognized none. These men had come from the surrounding towns. They must have marched all night.

Andrew continued walking. He didn't want to stop, didn't want to get caught in the talk of another raid. He was still exhausted from the night before, and it was miserable outside as a freezing rain fell. He needed time alone. The image of Joseph hauling down the King's colors was burned into Andrew's brain. And Jack! Jack had called him a traitor!

Andrew had ignored the knock on the door in the early morning hours. Looking down from his upstairs window, he had seen a figure but was not certain it was Joseph until he heard him call out to open the door. Andrew left the window and returned to his bed, pretending not to be home. He didn't want to talk. He felt numb. Joseph pounded on the door a few more times before there was silence.

Now, Andrew looked down the street. Coming toward him were a group of boys from school. One was Charles Cutter. Andrew hoped they hadn't seen him. He didn't want to talk to any of the boys. And, he did not want to talk to Charles Cutter.

What would Dr. Cutter think of what he did? What would Hannah think? They were friends of Governor Wentworth. Hannah thought the world of the governor. His plans of going to Harvard and practicing medicine suddenly seemed far away. His stomach felt queasy.

Andrew ducked into the State House through a side entrance. The first floor was empty as he stepped through the heavy wooden door. He closed it behind him and leaned against it. For just a few minutes, he could be alone. He needed more time to think before everyone else told him what to think.

The streets were full of men, many spilling into the taverns, but they wouldn't enter the State House. Unauthorized public meetings were forbidden in the State House. He chuckled at the irony. The men on the street had looted King George's fort and had torn down his flag, but some rules were still followed.

But the peace and quiet was short lived.

Voices from above were clear now. There were men in the upstairs chamber.

Andrew recognized one voice. It was Governor Wentworth's.

"Major Sullivan," the governor began, his voice forceful, in command. "You are an officer of the militia. I personally gave you your commission." The governor's voice echoed through the building and Andrew froze. It sounded as if the governor was standing right next to him. "I demand that you disperse the men gathered in town. End this treasonous rebellion!"

Major Sullivan did not hesitate, his voice unwavering. "We have been informed that two regiments of British regulars have embarked from Boston and are on their way to take possession of His Majesty's Castle William and Mary. The action at the fort was self-defense. The provincial powder had to be protected. And," Sullivan continued, "it is our intention to seize the weapons and cannon at the fort before they can be put to use by the British regulars against us!"

Andrew shuddered. A second attack?

Major Sullivan did not relent. "The fort and its soldiers no longer are a source of protection for us," he declared. "We must protect ourselves from Captain Cochran, the soldiers at the fort and the regulars on the way."

Governor Wentworth retorted, "Major Sullivan, I am not aware that any regulars are being sent here to Portsmouth or to the Castle.

The message that Mr. Revere brought from Boston was nothing but a wicked falsehood!"

Andrew took in a sharp breath. Wicked falsehood? Was this possible?

The governor's voice was now filled with contempt as he said, "This was not some mistake by the committee in Boston. This vile report was intentional! Lies!"

Lies, a wicked falsehood? Andrew physically took a step back in the empty room as if he had been pushed. Could the committee from Boston have been wrong? Or worse? Could the information have been a lie, a falsehood as the governor claimed? Was it a calculated act to provoke the people to attack the fort? Could the committee from Boston have intentionally misled them? Had they raided the King's fort for no reason?

A coldness wrapped around Andrew like a blanket.

He heard heavy footsteps, then Governor Wentworth's voice boomed again, "Lies! It was a vile report calculated to alarm and lead the people into the most dangerous and destructive madness!"

Major Sullivan stammered, suddenly sounding unsure. "Why? Why would the committee from Boston spread such a lie?"

Sputtering in rage, Governor Wentworth shouted, "Why? Why? Why would they do such a thing, you ask? To serve their own purpose! To stir up the fine citizens in Portsmouth into acting as unreasonably as the Sons of Violence in Boston!"

Andrew heard pacing footsteps, then the governor thundered again, "Dumping the East India tea was a reckless destruction of property and a flagrant disregard for royal authority, but it pales in comparison to the actions taken yesterday! The participants in yesterday's raid committed treason!"

Andrew heard himself gasp. He reached up and covered his mouth with his hand. Treason. The governor had said the word. His legs felt weak. "Treason." He whispered the word in the silent first floor room. They had overpowered the soldiers, taken gunpowder and worse, they had hauled down the King's colors. It was treason. He could hang. Even Jack said so.

Major Sullivan spoke slowly, forcefully again, "It was a defensive act on the people's part. The citizens had no reason to doubt the information and every reason to believe it. Gage seized the powder outside of Boston. There's no reason he wouldn't take control of ours. We would be left at the mercy of the British regulars! That is unthinkable!"

Andrew exhaled slowly, his thoughts cleared. Major Sullivan was right. Why would they question the information from the committee of correspondence in Boston? The committees were formed to protect the colonists. General Gage had seized powder, already. Once they received the information, what choice did they have? If they hadn't acted, troops could use the gunpowder against the people in the Piscataqua region. There would be no way to protect against the British troops. Surely the governor would understand that they had no choice.

Governor Wentworth said, "Send your men home and restore the gunpowder." It was an order given by the royal governor of the province.

"Your Excellency," Major Sullivan spoke evenly, "I will ask the men to reconsider and go back to their homes, but I doubt they will listen to me. There are hundreds of men in the town who have come from their homes in surrounding communities to protect the citizens. These are not men who are simply looking for a fight. Many of these men are of property and wealth. Both of which they intend to keep."

"Major Sullivan, no one in the government is trying to take away any man's property or wealth."

There was silence for a moment before Major Sullivan said, "I will speak with the men and tell them this new information. I believe this may calm them. But we are now in a difficult position. The men who raided the fort did so in belief that the powder and weapons would be used against us. It was an act of self-defense. But as you now state, it could be viewed," he hesitated, "less favorably."

Andrew heard pacing footsteps. Then Major Sullivan spoke again, "Your Excellency, perhaps if you will issue a pardon for any man who participated in the raid of the Castle, the crowd will disperse."

Andrew saw a ray of hope in the request. He was glad Major Sullivan was presenting their case to the governor. A pardon was the answer. A pardon would forgive the raiders for the actions taken at the fort, including hauling down the King's colors. He held his breath waiting for Governor Wentworth's response.

His response was immediate. "Major, as you are well aware, I can pardon many acts, but I cannot pardon treason. To attempt to do so would be a crime. As a public official, I cannot and I will not conceal the existence of treason."

Andrew put his hand on a support column to steady himself.

Major Sullivan tried to negotiate. "Or, if not a pardon, perhaps you can assure those responsible that they will not be prosecuted."

Governor Wentworth did not hesitate. "Major Sullivan, I want to be very clear. I can make no promises. Some of the matter is out of my hands. However, if the men return the gunpowder to the fort, disperse immediately and go home, I will present this information to His Majesty with hope that he will see that a wrong has been made right."

Major Sullivan said, "I will convey this information to the men."

THE STATE HOUSE
2:30 P.M.

☙ ☙ ☙

Hearing footsteps on the stairs, Andrew moved out of sight behind a large support column. Major Sullivan and Justice Samuel Penhallow thundered down the stairs and left through the large front door of the State House. Moments later, more footsteps echoed through the open hall. Andrew looked up to see Jack running down the stairs with a document in his hands, hurrying toward the side door.

Andrew stepped out from the shadows behind the pillar.

Jack stopped abruptly as he came face to face with his schoolmate.

"Andrew," Jack said in a half-whisper.

Andrew, relieved that Jack had not shouted out his name for the men above to hear, was suddenly hopeful that his school friend now understood the reason behind the assault on the fort. Major Sullivan had explained it well. The men that raided the fort did so to protect the citizens. But his hope evaporated as he looked at Jack's face.

Jack's eyes blazed as he spoke through clenched teeth, "What are you doing here?" Jack suddenly took a few aggressive steps toward Andrew, as if he might attack, but stopped short. He accused, "Are you spying now?"

"No!" Andrew stepped back, unsettled by Jack's uncharacteristic anger and suspicion. He knew Jack did not understand his actions.

"No! No! I just came in to get away from the men, outside."

Jack stared into Andrew's eyes as if unsure whether to believe him.

"Jack," Andrew spoke in a low voice. "You heard why we went to the fort. British regulars were coming. We had to secure the powder to protect ourselves."

Jack stepped toward Andrew again. "Protect yourselves? Who were you protecting yourselves from? My father? The soldiers at His Majesty's Castle William and Mary? From me? My father and the soldiers serve to protect you!"

His voice rose now and Andrew worried that the men above in the council chamber would hear.

"My father and the soldiers are the protectors of the citizens! You, Andrew Beckett, put the gunpowder into the hands of traitors!"

"No, Jack. We believed British regulars were on the way."

Jack was unwavering. "No soldiers were coming! My father is in command and will remain in command."

"We were told regulars were coming!"

Jack asked, "Do you believe what Governor Wentworth told Major Sullivan? You know the governor. Do you trust his word?"

Andrew considered the question. He did believe the governor. Even though some people didn't trust him, Andrew thought him a man of honor. The governor had explained why he sent carpenters to Boston when Charles Cutter asked about them. He was compelled to do so by a Royal Order. And he also felt it would maintain order. Order was essential to avoid chaos. That's what he'd said. He hadn't lied. He just didn't tell people what he was doing. Andrew did not think the governor would lie to Major Sullivan.

"Yes," he answered.

"Then make this right. Take the powder back to the fort as Governor Wentworth commanded!"

Jack marched to the side door. He turned and issued an order of his own, "Make it right Andrew Beckett!" He slammed the door as he left.

The State House was suddenly quiet and Andrew had never felt so alone.

Within minutes, the front door burst open and Major Sullivan and Justice Penhallow strode through. This time John Langdon and three other men were with them. The sound of their rapid footsteps echoed in the emptiness. Andrew stepped back into the shadows.

The men, deep in conversation, eyes cast downward had not seen him. They sprinted up the stairs to the governor's chamber.

"Your Excellency, may we have another moment of your time?" The voice was Sullivan's.

The governor's voice was calm. "I hope you have brought news that the men have chosen to see reason and have agreed to return the powder to His Majesty's Castle and disperse immediately."

Major Sullivan spoke, "The men are still intent upon a return to the Castle. Governor, you must understand that we view this action as required for self-preservation. But if you agree to pardon the men—"

The governor cut him off. "I cannot grant a pardon for treason! You attacked the King's fort. You hauled down the King's colors! The best I can offer is that I will recommend to His Majesty that he show mercy if the powder is returned immediately and if the men leave the streets of Portsmouth."

"Your Excellency, you must understand that the men who took the powder and weapons acted in good faith. They believed we would be attacked by the regulars."

Governor Wentworth's voice was tight. "I assured you that the communiqué delivered by Mr. Revere was false. Regulars were not dispatched to Portsmouth or to the fort. There are no troops in the streets — only wayward men from this province!" Anger rising, the governor raged, "It is the height of absurdity to think this little colony could oppose the vengeance of Great Britain! If you continue with this insult upon the government, you will not escape its just resentment for an insult on its honor! Tell the men to return the powder immediately and then disperse and return home. I will hear no more!"

Andrew heard footsteps descending the staircase as he slipped out the side door.

The crowd outside the State House was even larger than when he entered. "Storm the fort! Storm the fort! Storm the fort!" the crowd chanted. Anger and frustration filled the faces of the men that blanketed the street.

The chant continued for several minutes.

"Quiet! Quiet! We must have quiet!" It was John Langdon.

Major Sullivan and John Langdon stood on the steps of the State House. Both men gazed out over the masses standing shoulder to shoulder in the freezing rain. Andrew worked his way through the swarming men.

"Storm the fort! Storm the fort! Storm the fort!" the chant continued.

Other shouts filtered through.

"Let him talk!"

"Quiet!"

Major Sullivan raised his arm and the crowd slowly fell silent. He told them, "We have spoken with Governor Wentworth. He has assured us that the communication delivered by Mr. Revere was not accurate. He has stated that no regulars are on the way to His Majesty's Castle William and Mary."

"Lies!" someone shouted.

Anger erupted in the crowd. Andrew was jostled as men surged forward, pushing him with them.

"The governor is lying! It's a trap!"

A man standing next to Andrew called out, "No troops on the way? What did we do?"

Another yelled, "We attacked the fort for no reason!"

Rage and confusion raced through the men. Andrew could not tell who was angrier, those who thought the governor was lying, or those who believed they had needlessly attacked His Majesty's Castle William and Mary.

Shouts continued from all sides.

John Langdon tried to quiet the crowd again, but with no success. Jeers and insults hurled through the air.

"Quiet!" It was Major Sullivan. He waited for the crowd to let him speak. "The governor said to return the powder."

"NO!" the shouts rose in the air.

"We need not take any action tonight!" Major Sullivan called out over the protests.

A man close to Andrew jeered, "We can't take the powder back!"

Men all around shouted in agreement.

Langdon stepped forward now and waved for quiet again. "We will vote right now that all participants involved in yesterday's action at the fort did so for the protection of the people of New Hampshire! We can protect ourselves. All agree?"

"YEA!" The response thundered from the men in the street.

"Opposed?"

Silence.

"Go home for now." Major Sullivan ordered.

Andrew hung back on the edge of the crowd.

John Langdon hurried down the steps of the State House into the crowd of men and walked in Andrew's direction. Just as he reached Andrew, a man rushed forward. Andrew recognized him immediately. It was Chief Justice Atkinson.

Stopping Langdon, Atkinson grabbed his arm and leaned into Langdon's face. "Flee the country or your head will swing from a gallows rope before the end of the week!"

Andrew's blood ran cold. The Chief Justice was announcing the sentence for the crime committed not only by John Langdon, but all who participated in the raid. Swing from a gallows rope.

Andrew did not hear Mr. Langdon's response, but men rushed forward toward Langdon and the Chief Justice. One declared, "John Langdon will be protected at the expense of our lives!"

Cheers followed as the men surrounded Langdon.

With a wave of his hand, John Langdon turned toward Broad Street to the home he shared with his brother Woodbury.

Following Langdon's lead, many men left the Parade. But about forty men, many from Durham, stayed close to Major Sullivan. Others tarried as well. Major Sullivan, along with a large number of men walked toward Tilton's Tavern.

TILTON'S TAVERN
3:00 P.M.

♛ ♛ ♛

Andrew stayed close to the Durham men. They entered Tilton's Tavern. But before Andrew could pass through the doorway, he was yanked backward.

"Where have you been?" It was Joseph. "I went to your house after coming back to town from taking powder inland. Then I went back a couple of hours ago."

"What do you want?" Andrew was abrupt. Now, standing before him, all he could see was Joseph hauling down the King's flag and cheering in victory. Andrew did not feel victorious.

Joseph was agitated. He spoke quickly, "Come with me. Mr. Langdon is taking charge." He nodded to a group of men down the street. "Several of us are going with Mr. Langdon to make a plan to raid the fort tonight." Joseph's eyes were wide "We have to get the cannons. We may even raid the Treasury!"

"No." Andrew was certain. "I'm not going anywhere with you."

"Drew, we can't give up now! Not now!"

140

"Give up what? No soldiers were on the way! We know that! Governor Wentworth isn't lying. If regulars had been coming, they would be here by now!"

Joseph's contempt was now aimed at Andrew. "I thought you were with us. I thought you were strong enough to do what was right!"

Andrew's anger was barely contained. "I went to the fort to secure the powder for the province because we received word that regulars would seize it and we couldn't get more! I went to help protect the people of the province! I thought that was right!" Andrew didn't stop to breathe. "All we had to do was take the powder. That was enough to protect the people. That was the plan! But you declared war on King George! You hauled down the King's flag! I saw you!"

"Drew," Joseph sighed in seeming frustration. "As soon as Cochran refused to hand over the powder peacefully we *all* attacked King George's fort! There is no turning back!"

Andrew glared at Joseph.

"Come with us!" Joseph implored. "Even if the troops aren't on the way, what do you think will happen to us now? The British government closed the port in Boston just because some men threw tea overboard. We attacked King George's fort! The British government will destroy us!"

Andrew shook his head, rejecting Joseph's words. Everything was so confused. He had gone to the fort for the right reason, but now—

Joseph grabbed Andrew by both shoulders and shoved him into the clapboard wall of Tilton's Tavern, pinning him. Joseph's eyes

141

mere slits as he seethed, "Don't even think about returning the powder! Without powder, we have no chance of protecting ourselves!"

Andrew shoved his body forward with all his might, pushing Joseph backward. "I'll decide what I think!"

Joseph took a step back, his voice quiet. "Face what is happening before it is too late. Decide Drew." He turned and walked away.

Andrew straightened his mussed clothing, smoothed his hair and walked away from Joseph and into Tilton's Tavern.

The mood inside the tavern was mainly subdued. Andrew sat down at a table by a window. Major Sullivan sat at a table across from him. He looked tired, his cheeks ruddy against his dark complexion.

"We should head home to Durham," a man said. "I don't see the point of getting mixed up in this any further if troops are not on the way."

Major Sullivan seemed to agree. He told them, "Governor Wentworth assured me that the report from the Boston committee was wrong. I have no reason to doubt his word. The men who participated in the raid acted only because they believed British regulars were on the way. If they had not been told the falsehood, this raid would not have occurred."

Another said, "They may have decided to remove the powder anyway based on the King's order restricting arms and powder."

Major Sullivan agreed. "True, but cooler heads may have handled it in a different manner."

A man with his back to Andrew said, "The Chief Justice said that Langdon and the others committed treason."

The tall man in the group said, "We helped hide the powder. We could swing from the gallows too if we don't return it."

That set off a rumble of agreement among the men.

Andrew sat back in silent fear. It was true. If they didn't return the powder, they could all swing from the gallows. He knew there was no way he could escape the punishment. Captain Cochran would identify him as one of the raiders.

A large punch bowl was placed on Major Sullivan's table. The men filled their mugs and continued to talk. A bowl was placed on Andrew's table as more men came through the doorway.

Andrew glanced around. The tavern was filling up now. Three men sat down at his table and nodded a greeting. Andrew didn't know them. Except for Major Sullivan, he didn't recognize any face in the tavern. But, he listened to what the men had to say.

As the men drank, many saw less reason to raid the fort again. Even those who initially insisted that Governor Wentworth was lying about the troops had to admit that the regulars would have arrived by now.

Major Sullivan was leaning toward sending the men inside Tilton's Tavern back to their homes, but they had not yet decided whether to return the powder to the fort or not. Andrew's head throbbed as he tried to come to terms with the fact that he could be charged with treason.

Then a man rose and asked to speak. As the room quieted, he identified himself as Captain Andrew McClary from Epsom. He told the men in the tavern, "We must finish what we started."

There was a long silence as the men considered the statement.

"I agree with Captain McClary," a man Andrew didn't know finally said. "We'll appear weak if we end it here."

The reaction to his statement was mixed with cheers and grumbles.

Another man stood. "I don't think it is weak to end it. We thought regulars were on the way. They weren't. Anything we do now makes this bad situation worse."

This time there was more approval than jeers echoing through the room.

A man in Sullivan's group spoke up, "Troops may not have been on the way, but the other part of the express was correct."

The room was quiet again. The troops were the reason the fort was raided, but the man was right. The express contained more information.

He continued. "Gentlemen, we must not forget that a Royal Order has been issued prohibiting the export of gunpowder to the colonies."

"Yes!" a voice called out. "King George is preparing for war against us! He wants to be certain we cannot fight him! He and his regulars will crush us! What other reason could there be for not allowing us free access to powder?"

The room heated up, with shouts of agreement. The subdued mood changed as men talked among themselves.

"We need to alert as many as possible!"

A man near the door said, "Men from the Hamptons, Rye and New Castle are here, but expresses need to go out immediately to Exeter, Kingston, Nottingham—"

Another voice cut in, adding to the list, "Berwick, Kittery, York."

The room was filled with men shouting back and forth. Many believed that a second raid was wise while others still doubted that it was the right action to take.

The smell of sweat, smoke and ale blanketed the small space, but Andrew didn't move. As he listened he thought Joseph was right about one thing. Andrew had to pick a side.

HIS MAJESTY'S CASTLE WILLIAM AND MARY
10:00 P.M.

♕ ♕ ♕

Ephraim Hall stood guard. Eyes forward, his body tense. He rotated his injured shoulder, grimacing with every movement.

Jack stood next to him gripping his musket so tightly his fingers ached. Captain Cochran had not argued when Jack asked that he be included on the duty schedule after receiving an express that men were once again on their way to the Castle, this time led by Major John Sullivan.

The soldiers were ready. And, Jack's grandfather joined them. He arrived late the night before.

James Cochran stood at attention, musket in hand, on top of the platform on the wall next to the gate. Determination was etched into his deeply lined face. Jack had overheard his grandfather tell his son, Jack's father, to fight any raiders to the death.

Jack counted in silence, one, two, three . . . breathe. His body shivered from cold and anger. He seethed just thinking about how they were overrun by the very men they protect. The insult still stung.

But he held out some hope that the men planned to return the powder, particularly since the express said Major Sullivan led the men tonight. Jack had been present when Governor Wentworth ordered Major Sullivan, a militiaman, to return the powder.

Jack shifted his musket. The waiting was almost unbearable.

Isaac suddenly called out in the stillness. "Barges and boats!"

Ephraim turned toward the Piscataqua River. Jack did too.

Then Isaac shouted, "There are more men than before!"

Ephraim looked over at Jack and shook his head. Jack understood. Returning the powder would not require more men than the night before. These men were there to attack His Majesty's Castle. Jack felt his anger rise.

Ephraim shouted to Isaac. "Go get the captain."

Within moments Jack heard the men approaching. Their voices were loud and menacing. But Jack's grandfather didn't waiver. He shouted to the soldiers, "We'll fight to the death!"

Jack looked out over the mob gathering outside the fort and shuddered knowing if they fought, it could be to the death this time. In the distance, he saw that hundreds of men swarmed toward them.

Ephraim's voice boomed, warning the approaching men. "Stay back from the gate!"

Major Sullivan stopped the men a short distance from the gate of Castle William and Mary.

"Who goes there?" Ephraim Hall demanded. His voice, strong despite the frightening mob of angry men before them.

The Major stepped forward. "I am Major John Sullivan, Militia. I wish to speak with Captain Cochran."

Jack's eyes remained fixed on the men as Captain Cochran climbed up on the platform by the gate. In the moonlight his face was expressionless. He did not give them any satisfaction by showing fear despite the fact that he had no ability to protect the fort.

Boldly Captain Cochran asked, "Have you come to return His Majesty's gunpowder, Major Sullivan?"

Sneering laughter bubbled up from the men below.

"Captain, we have come to take possession of provincial property," Sullivan told him. "It is my understanding that the purpose of this fort is to protect us, the citizens."

The captain retorted angrily. "You have no authority! You are mere rebels!"

Major Sullivan spoke again, "Sir, these rebels as you call us are men of property, not rabble as you wish to believe. We are all citizens who deserve protection from our government, not threats!"

Captain Cochran did not speak immediately. His eyes searched the jeering raiders again. Then he spoke. This time his voice was quieter, "Major, you say you and your men wish only to seize that which belongs to the province."

"That is correct."

"If that is the case, I will allow your men to take provincial property. However, under no circumstances will I allow them to remove any property belonging to His Majesty."

"What property would that be?" Sullivan called back from the darkness.

"I will allow a committee of three men to come inside the installation and I will show them the provincial property you may take."

Jack watched as the men talked among themselves. He didn't like the idea of relinquishing the provincial property. They protected the provincial property for the people. But, Jack understood that they had no ability to protect provincial property or the King's property from so many men. Perhaps they would be satisfied with taking the provincial property only.

Three men now approached the gate. They identified themselves as Andrew McClary, Jeremiah Bryant and Thomas Stevenson. Captain Cochran nodded to Isaac and he opened the hastily repaired gate and the men entered the fort.

"Jack," his father called to him, "Come with me."

Jack left his position and accompanied his father. They showed the men the provincial property consisting of about fifty old muskets. The man named Bryant questioned whether there was more that belonged to the province, but Captain Cochran showed the men the King's mark on a number of cannons and assured them that all else in the fort belonged to the King or was the personal property of the Cochran family.

They returned to the gate and Captain Cochran told them, "I will allow the muskets I showed you to be peacefully removed by ten men, no more."

Captain Cochran warned them, "The men selected must not disturb or take any items belonging to the King."

McClary remained inside the fort with the captain. As the other two left the fort interior, Jack repositioned on the wall and watched.

The men met quickly with Major Sullivan and ten moved to the gate. Captain Cochran ordered, "Open the gate."

Isaac partially opened the battered gate.

But, suddenly the mob pushed through the opening. Isaac was knocked to the ground as the men surged. He scrambled to his feet and swung his weapon into position. He now pointed his musket at the men and appeared to struggle not to fire.

Jack held his position and turned his musket on the raiders.

"Hold your fire!" Captain Cochran shouted.

Jack continued to point his weapon at the men invading the fort, ready to shoot on command.

James Cochran, Jack's grandfather called out, "Traitors! You are nothing but liars and traitors!" as the mob poured through the gate of His Majesty's Castle William and Mary.

"Hold your fire!" Captain Cochran shouted, again, "Hold your fire!"

Jack lowered his musket and watched as Piscataqua men swarmed into the fort, breaking down what was left of the gate.

Once inside, men ran in all directions, and Jack knew there was no way to stop them.

It was then that Jack saw Andrew.

Jack dropped down off the platform, outraged to see Andrew. He shouted angrily, "Traitor! I can't believe you defied Governor Wentworth's order to restore the powder!"

"Jack!" Andrew pushed through the sea of men. He wanted to talk to him. He wanted Jack to understand.

"Jack!" Andrew finally reached him. "Listen to me. We have to take all of the weapons. It is the only way we can protect ourselves."

Jack's eyes blazed with rage. He shouted into Andrew's face,

"Governor Wentworth said no soldiers were coming! Revere's warning was false! You said you believed Governor Wentworth!"

Andrew tried again to explain. "I believed what Governor Wentworth said. I believe no troops were on the way, yesterday, when we took the powder. I believe the committee of correspondence in Boston made a mistake."

Jack's face was now a mix of anger and confusion. "But, if you knew no troops were on the way, why didn't you return the powder like Governor Wentworth ordered? Why didn't you make this right?"

Andrew said, "Because the government is trying to keep us from getting powder to protect ourselves. And because I believe troops *are* on the way now."

Jack stared at Andrew in silence.

Andrew continued, "I respect Governor Wentworth and I'm certain he met his responsibility as governor. As royal governor of the province he is required to maintain order. Because of that, I'm certain he called for troops to protect the fort after it was raided yesterday."

Andrew studied Jack's face as he asked, "Don't you see, Jack? We couldn't bring the powder back. We have to keep the powder we took, and we have to seize the weapons to protect ourselves from the troops that are now on the way. Governor Wentworth had to call for assistance. He had to maintain order. As royal governor, he is bound to do so."

Jack did not answer. He recalled the governor's words that he would take action.

Andrew said, " There is no choice now. We have to take everything at the fort or the troops will use the weapons against us."

Jack leaned forward his face within inches of Andrew's. Through clenched teeth he said, "Andrew Beckett, you are a traitor!"

Andrew watched Jack walk away from him and wondered if Jack would ever understand.

"Over here!" came a shout nearby.

Andrew turned to see men trying to move a cannon. It was a four-pounder that clearly displayed the King's mark. He looked in Jack's direction one more time then went to help.

"I heard there are fifteen four-pounders and a nine pounder that we need to take from the fort," a man from the group said.

A sturdy man replied, "I heard John Langdon is keeping watch in Portsmouth and will send word if the troops arrive. We will get what we can. We'll work through the night. Colonel Nathaniel Folsom from Exeter is on the way to Portsmouth with more men."

Andrew looked up as he pushed the heavy cannon toward the gate. Men were seizing anything they could carry — muskets, bayonets, small arms and cannon shot.

Looking to the right, he saw Joseph watching him. He'd not seen Joseph since their confrontation outside of the tavern. Joseph held up his hand in a quick wave. Andrew gave a slight nod. It was all he could manage — at least for now.

Andrew turned back to work with the men to move the cannon. As he pushed the cannon, he tried to push his angry feelings out of his mind. Right now he needed to help secure the weapons for the colonists in the region. But those feelings crept in.

Andrew was angry that Joseph, and the others who pulled down the flag, made a bad situation worse. And he was angry that Jack refused to see that the choice was made for the men who now raided the fort — not by them.

But mostly, Andrew was angry that the British government was trying to force the colonists to submit to unfair policies that benefitted the Empire but trampled on the colonists' rights as British citizens.

What the future would bring, Andrew did not know.

He pushed the cannon with all of his might, angry that he was forced to raid His Majesty's Castle William and Mary.

He knew, though, he had no choice.

AFTERWORD

♛ ♛ ♛

The communication delivered by Paul Revere was not entirely correct. British troops had not been ordered to take over Fort William and Mary, but at least one ship of the Royal Navy was, in fact, headed to the Piscataqua. At the time of the raids, Governor Wentworth was aware that the British admiral in Boston had ordered a warship to Portsmouth. Its assignment was to prohibit the smuggling of arms and ammunition into the colony. And as Andrew expected, Governor Wentworth did request assistance on December 14th, after the initial attack on the fort. In a letter to General Gage he wrote in part:

> SIR....
>
> It is with the utmost concern I am called upon by my duty to the King to communicate to your Excellency a most un-happy affair perpetrated here this day . . . about four hundred men were collected together, and immediately proceeded to his Majesty's Castle, William and Mary, at the entrance of this harbor, and forcibly took possession thereof . . . and by violence carried away upwards of one hundred barrels of

powder belonging to the King, deposited in the castle. I am informed that expresses have been circulated through the neighboring towns, to collect a number of people tomorrow, or as soon as possible, to carry away all the cannon and arms belonging to the castle which they will undoubtedly effect, unless some assistance should arrive from Boston in time to prevent it. . . Neither is the Province or custom house treasury in any degree safe, if it should come into the mind of the popular leaders to seize upon them.

The principal persons who took the lead in this enormity are well known. Upon the best information I can obtain, this mischief originates from the publishing of the Secretary of State's letter, and the King's order in Council at Rhode Island, prohibiting the exportation of military stores from Great Britain . . . before which all was perfectly quiet and peaceable here. I am etc.

(Signed)   J.WENTWORTH

On December 17th the sloop *Canceaux* arrived in Portsmouth followed by the frigate *Scarborough* two days later. The ships carried fifty to one hundred Royal Marines. But by the time the ships arrived, the weapons retrieved during the second raid including 16 cannons, and 82 to 94 muskets had been successfully taken into the interior of New Hampshire — out of the reach of the King's Troops.

Governor John Wentworth's authority was greatly weakened after the event. Four months later, shots were fired in Lexington and Concord, Massachusetts.

AUTHOR NOTES

ॐ ॐ ॐ

While writing this book, minor liberties were taken regarding time and place to enable the characters to fully experience the events and to move the story forward. However, there was one major exception. Captain Chiver's attempt to transport sheep occurred in November of 1774 — not in December.

And, as stated in the preface, Andrew Beckett, Jack Cochran and Joseph Reed are fictional characters created to represent the differing viewpoints held by the people of the Piscataqua region at the time. However except for those three characters, all named individuals were real people whose lives were impacted by the events in December 1774.

Below are highlights of some of their lives after the raid at Castle William and Mary.

• John Langdon served as an agent for the Congress during the Revolutionary War, responsible for building Continental ships. He later served multiple terms as governor of New Hampshire and was elected to the U. S. Senate.

- John Sullivan was a general in the Continental Army during the Revolutionary War and twice served as governor of New Hampshire.

- Dr. Ammi Ruhamah Cutter was Physician General of the Eastern Department of the Continental Army. After the war he returned to private practice in Portsmouth and was president of the New Hampshire Medical Society.

- Charles Cutter eventually attended Harvard College, but he is believed to have drowned at the age of sixteen while crossing Fresh Pond in Cambridge, Massachusetts. The other named Cutter children remained in Portsmouth.

- John and Frances Wentworth, along with their infant son Charles, fled their home in Portsmouth in June of 1775. John Wentworth later served as governor of Nova Scotia.

- Captain John Cochran remained loyal to the British government and later settled in Canada with his wife and children.

- Little is known about the Cochran children. Sally and Nancy likely lived at the fort at the time of the raid, but William may have been too young. There is a record of a young (perhaps teenaged) John Cochran at the fort, but it is not clear if he was a son or another relative of the family.

- Major Samuel Hale continued to teach at the Latin Grammar School until the late 1780's.

Terri A. DeMitchell

Interesting Facts:

- The New Hampshire motto is Live Free or Die.
- The New Hampshire State Constitution still provides for revolution:

[Art.] 10. [Right of Revolution.] Government being in-stituted for the common benefit, protection, and security, of the whole community, and not for the private interest or emolument of any one man, family, or class of men; there-fore, whenever the ends of government are perverted, and public liberty manifestly endangered, and all other means of redress are ineffectual, the people may, and of right ought to reform the old, or establish a new government. The doctrine of nonresistance against arbitrary power, and oppression, is absurd, slavish, and destructive of the good and happiness of mankind.   June 2, 1784

SELECTED BIBLIOGRAPHY

※ ※ ※

BOOKS

Divine, Robert A. et al. *America Past & Present Volume 1 to 1877*. New York: Pearson Longman, 2007.

Hackett, David Fischer. *Paul Revere's Ride*. New York: Oxford University Press, 1994.

Mayo, Lawrence Shaw. *John Langdon of New Hampshire*. Port Washington: Kennikat Press, 1937.

Mayo, Lawrence Shaw. *John Wentworth Governor of New Hampshire: 1767-1775*. Cambridge: Harvard University Press, 1921.

Rakove, Jack. *Revolutionaries*. Boston: Houghton Mifflin Harcourt, 2010.

Sammons, Mark J. and Cunningham, Valerie. *Black Portsmouth*. Durham: University of New Hampshire Press, 2004.

Whittemore, Charles. *A General of the Revolution: John Sullivan of New Hampshire*. New York: Columbia University Press, 1961.

Wilderson, Paul W. *Governor John Wentworth & the American Revolution: The English Connection*. Durham: University of New Hampshire

Press, 1994.

   Winslow, Richard E. *The Piscataqua Gundalow: Workhorse for a Tidal Basin Empire*. Portsmouth: Portsmouth Marine Society, 1983

ARTICLES

   "Stoodley's Tavern". http://www.strawberybanke.org/

   Brewster, Charles W. "Tales of the Old Bell Tavern". http://www.seacoastnh.com/

   Garvin, James L. "Colonial Statehouse Through Time". http://seacoastnh.com/

   Kehr, Thomas F. (2012). "The Seizure of His Majesty's Fort William and Mary at New Castle, New Hampshire, December 14-15, 1774". http://www.nhssar.org/essays/FortConstitution.htm (Also on file at the New Hampshire Historical Society.)

   Kehr, Thomas F. (2007). "Some Participants in the Raids on Fort William and Mary." http://www.nhssar.org/essays/Namelist.htm (Also on file at the New Hampshire Historical Society.)

LETTERS

   Cochran, John. (1774). Report of John Cochran, Captain of Fort William & Mary, to Governor Wentworth. From: American Archives, Vol. 1, p. 1042, Appendix to *Belnap's History of New Hampshire, (1812), Vol. lll*, p. 330; *N. H. Provincial Papers, Vol. Vll.* p 420. (http://www.library.unh.edu/special/index.php/exhibits/capture-of-fort-william-and-mary/cochran1)

Wentworth, John (1774). Letter to General Gage. From: American Archives, Vol. 1, p. 1042, Appendix to *Belnap's History of New Hampshire (1812), Vol. lll*, p. 328; *N. H. Provincial Papers, Vol. Vll*, p 420. (http://www.library.unh.edu/special/index.php/exhibits/capture-of-fort-william-and-mary/wentworth1)